Doroth...

If Mission Creek i... ...er of Hades in a handba... ...quilt know what is happening. 'Tis the season for losing your valuables! First Luke Callaghan abandons us, and now our scrumptious D.A., Spence Harrison, has disappeared! In addition, Nadine Delarue claims she lost her diamond solitaire, but something tells us that new pooch of hers might have needed some extra crunch in his dog food.

By the way, let's see a show of hands for those who think Josie Carson (née Lavender) might be overdoing it with "eating for two." Isn't there a limit to how much you're supposed to gain during pregnancy? Whatever the case may be, Josie, that extra baby weight sure looks good on you!

I'm pleased to announce that Dylan Bridges is the winner of our Yellow Rose Café Wednesday raffle.

...quilt made by our very own "Over Eighty" quilting circle. Dylan, ignore some of the irregular stitching patterns and remember that there's enough room under that quilt for you and that beautiful wife of yours. All raffle proceeds go to benefit the Mission Creek High School marching band and their tour of New York City.

And that's all she wrote for this issue, members. As always, make your best stop of the day right here at the Lone Star Country Club!

About the Author

LONE STAR
LSCC
COUNTRY CLUB
EST. 1923

DIXIE BROWNING

is an award-winning painter and writer, mother and grandmother. Her father was a big-league baseball player, her grandfather a sea captain. In addition to nearly ninety-five contemporary romances, Dixie and her sister, Mary Williams, have written more than a dozen historical romances under the name Bronwyn Williams.

Among her romances, very few have been set in Texas. Even so, despite having lived in North Carolina her entire life, she was tempted by the offer to write one of the LONE STAR COUNTRY CLUB books. Long a fan of suspense, she was especially drawn to that particular aspect of the series. New tactics were required to deal with the many continuity elements. Some things, however, transcend location. If you agree that she's succeeded in rising to the challenge, perhaps you can reassure her through her Web site, www.dixiebrowning.com, or at: P.O. Box 1389, Buxton, NC 27920.

DIXIE
BROWNING

THE QUIET
SEDUCTION

Silhouette Books

Published by Silhouette Books

America's Publisher of Contemporary Romance

Special thanks and acknowledgment are given
to Dixie Browning for her contribution
to the LONE STAR COUNTRY CLUB series.

SILHOUETTE BOOKS

ISBN 0-373-61357-1

THE QUIET SEDUCTION

Printed in U.S.A.

Welcome to the

LONE STAR

LSCC

COUNTRY CLUB

EST. 1923

Where Texas society reigns supreme—
and appearances are everything.

The Texas mafia is on the warpath....

Spence Harrison: While en route to the state prison, this high-powered D.A. saw a little boy in harm's way of a tornado. It wasn't a question whether he'd heroically risk his life to save the lad. But hitting his head and suffering amnesia wasn't part of the plan. Neither was seducing the boy's soft-spoken mom, whose tender ministrations penetrated Spence's guarded heart....

Ellen Wagner: This struggling farmer didn't know what to make of the wounded stranger who made her pulse race out of control. But when menacing men came looking for her handsome housemate, she instinctively knew she had to protect him. Will their newfound love be darkened by the Texas underworld?

Mayhem in Mission Creek: During a power struggle between two formidable mobsters, a shocking suspicion comes to light about a presumed-dead heiress. Now the truth sets off a dangerous chain of events....

THE FAMILIES

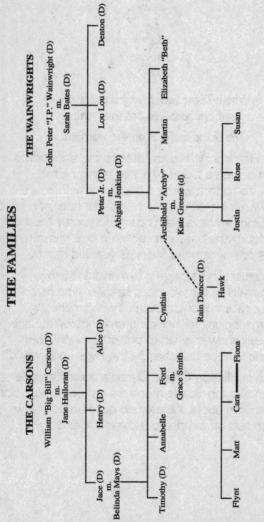

THE CARSONS

William "Big Bill" Carson (D)
m.
Jane Halloran (D)

- Jace (D)
  m.
  Belinda Mays (D)
- Henry (D)
- Alice (D)

Timothy (D) — Annabelle — Ford — Cynthia
m.
Grace Smith

Flynt — Matt — Cara ▬ Fiona

THE WAINWRIGHTS

John Peter "J.P." Wainwright (D)
m.
Sarah Bates (D)

- Peter Jr. (D)
  m.
  Abigail Jenkins (D)
- Lou Lou (D)
- Denton (D)

Archibald "Archy" — Martin — Elizabeth "Beth"
m.
Kate Greene (d)

Justin — Rose — Susan

Rain Dancer (D)

Hawk

D Deceased
d Divorced
m. Married
---- Affair
▬ Twins

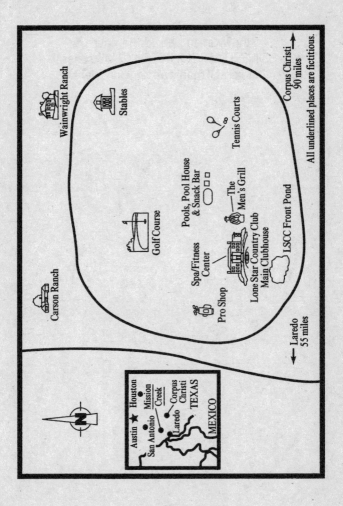

Wainwright Ranch

Carson Ranch

Stables

Golf Course

Pools, Pool House
& Snack Bar

The
Men's Grill

Tennis Courts

Spa/Fitness
Center

Lone Star Country Club
Main Clubhouse

Pro Shop

LSCC Front Pond

Laredo
55 miles

Corpus Christi
90 miles

All underlined places are fictitious.

TEXAS

Austin ★ Houston

Mission
Creek

San Antonio Corpus Christi

Laredo

MEXICO

N

To my editor, Margaret Marbury,
the woman behind the entire
LONE STAR COUNTRY CLUB series.
Margaret, I'm in awe of your talent.

One

Spence Harrison scanned the dial in search of a weather update while he drove, half his attention on the highway, half on the sky. He had enough on his mind without heading into a patch of nasty weather. In this section of South Texas, scattered showers might mean anything from a few tepid drops to baseball-size hail. Yesterday's prediction of scattered showers had produced a deluge.

Luckily, traffic was light on the secondary highway. All he had to do was watch out for slow-moving tractors and a speeding ticket, as his foot tended to be heavier on the accelerator when he was under tension. For a district attorney on his way to the state prison to take an on-site deposition—one he didn't trust anyone else to take—a speeding ticket would be embarrassing, to say the least.

Reaching up, he loosened his tie and unbuttoned his collar. Damn, it was getting hot! He turned the air conditioner up another notch. Cutting back to a moderate sixty-five miles an hour, he tried to concentrate on the task ahead. The trouble came in trying to narrow his focus.

The last call he'd taken before leaving his office had had nothing to do with the murder trial he was preparing to prosecute, or even the information he was hoping to uncover from this particular witness. Instead it con--

cerned Luke Callaghan, a good friend, Virginia Military Institute classmate and old marine corps buddy who had dropped off the radar screen after arriving in Central America. It had been more than a week since he'd reported in.

Considering his usual extravagant lifestyle, his disappearance would not have been surprising, but in this particular case it was definitely a cause for alarm. Luke was involved in a risky undercover rescue mission. Their former commander, Phillip Westin, had gone down somewhere in a Central American jungle—not a great place to go missing. Spence wasn't privy to all the details, but from the few he did know he'd been able to extrapolate others with his well-honed power of deduction. A logical mind and the ability to reason were valuable tools in his particular line of work.

At the moment, however, those abilities were being stretched thin. As the miles sped past, Spence's thoughts ricocheted back and forth between Luke's situation and recent revelations on an entirely different front that made it imperative that he find out just which cops had gone rogue. It was hardly the thing a man could ask if he wanted to stay healthy. At this point, not even Internal Affairs was above suspicion.

Spence could count on the fingers of one hand the cops he could trust. It was a sad state of affairs, damned sad. Most were probably clean, but he couldn't be sure. Not until he had enough evidence to trigger an outside investigation. He was counting on today's deposition to add a few more parts to the puzzle.

It had been the murder of Judge Carl Bridges that had shaken things loose. The judge had been a powerful man in Lone Star County—a man who had influenced countless lives, Spence's included. The two had met at a time when Spence had been headed down a dead-end road. He'd been no stranger to juvenile court. Thanks to Carl Bridges he had turned around, worked his tail off, and now, a couple of decades later, had a respectable career as a district attorney to show for it.

It was the judge's recent murder that had driven Spence on a mission of his own. Alex Black's fingerprints might have been all over the murder weapon, but someone else had to be pulling his strings. Black wasn't bright enough to act on his own. Spence was all but certain the punk was being set up to take the fall. He had a pretty good idea who was behind it, but certainty wasn't enough. He needed irrefutable evidence, and getting that evidence was not going to be easy. Under the circumstances, it might even be hazardous.

There had been a few questionable incidents recently that, taken singly, meant little. The car that had nearly run him off the road last week, he'd put down to a DUI. He'd immediately called the highway patrol, but by the time they'd arrived on the scene, the jerk had evidently gone to earth.

The hang-up calls he'd been receiving late at night he'd put down to kids's pranks. Even taken together, the incidents weren't conclusive-enough evidence that the mob wanted him out of the picture to put their own man in place. He happened to know, however, that they had their own candidate waiting in the wings should Spence decide to take early retirement.

On the surface Joe Ed Malone's credentials were impeccable, educationally, socially and politically. Scratch the surface, though, and he was as corrupt as they came. The mob owned him, from his custom-made toupee right down to his bench-made boots.

Spence had evidence in a hidden file, hoping he wouldn't have to use it, as it implicated several prominent citizens.

God, it was getting hot! Was this the end of November or the Fourth of July? Setting the AC on Arctic Blast, he angled the vents to blow in his face. The fact that he was running late didn't help. He should have taken the interstate, but he had some thinking to do and he couldn't concentrate with a fleet of eighteen-wheelers bearing down on his rear bumper.

Once again he checked his watch, then glanced nervously at the sky. Was it only his imagination or was that cloud up ahead several degrees darker?

Sighting a gas station, he checked his fuel gauge. Better to stop now than wait until he was hovering at empty. He should've filled up before he'd left town, but he'd had his mind on how to go about extracting the information he needed from a guy who probably didn't realize the significance of what he knew. Odds were better than even he wouldn't be able to pull it off, but it was worth a try. When a man was on a rat hunt, he couldn't afford to pass up a single dark hole.

After topping up his tank, Spence replaced his credit card in his wallet, slid the wallet back into the inside pocket of his suit jacket, then slung the coat onto the passenger seat atop his briefcase and portable tape recorder. Climbing back behind the wheel, he switched on the radio and hit the scan button, searching again for a weather forecast as he pulled back onto the highway.

Given a choice of farm reports, a cooking show or country music, he settled for Willie Nelson singing about an angel flying too close to the earth. There'd be break-in bulletins if any serious weather was headed this way.

He'd been driving less than five minutes when he noticed the ragged bottom of a particularly dark cloud rapidly moving toward him. Despite the heat, he felt a rash of cold prickles down his spine. Weather alert or no, he increased his speed. Not that he was all that eager to reach the state prison. He still hadn't quite decided on the best tactic to employ, but if things were about to turn nasty, there was a lot more security to be found behind those thick walls than on a wide-open stretch of highway in the middle of cow country. Black skies were bad; greenish-black skies were about seventeen degrees worse.

"Sweet Jesus," he muttered soulfully, glancing again through the side window. A moment later he began to swear in earnest as an all-too-familiar formation began to take shape. It was a funnel, all right. And unless one of them switched direction in the next few minutes, they were on a collision course.

It was then that Spence saw the boy on a bicycle a couple of hundred feet ahead. Poor kid was frozen, gawking at the twister racing toward him like steel to a magnet. Reflexes kicked in and Spence floored the accelerator, then slammed on the brakes. Not waiting for the car to stop fishtailing, he struggled to wrench open his door.

"Hit the dirt!" he screamed as he catapulted over the hood and dived at the figure standing immobile on the highway right-of-way. A chrome hubcap sailed out of nowhere, missing his head by inches. "Hit the ditch, hit the ditch!" he screamed again, tackling the kid and carrying them both into the drainage ditch just as a blinding wall of sand struck him in the face.

* * *

The sudden darkness was suffocating. Unfocused pain splintered through him, then there was nothing but noise and darkness. His first thought was that he was blind. Only gradually did disjointed fragments of awareness begin to drift past.

A kid maybe eight or nine years old... A kid on a bike beside the highway...

Echoes of a nasal tenor voice singing about...

Singing about something or other.

Lying half submerged in a swollen stream of muddy water, he made no effort to hang on to the images, the impressions, dimly aware that sooner or later something would snag and he'd be able to use it to pull himself up and get started on his way to—

To wherever.

In the sudden stillness he heard the sound of a woman's voice. She was shouting, crying.

Then something whimpered. A dog, maybe a kid.

Himself?

It sure as hell wasn't Willie Nelson, because he remembered Willie's voice. That was a start, wasn't it?

Something raked over his face. It hurt, and he tried to turn away.

Angel flying too close to the earth...

"Wait until I wipe off some of the mud. Don't try to open your eyes yet."

He opened his eyes. Tears flushed away some of the grit and he blinked away the dirty film to stare up at the haggard-looking angel leaning over him. She was holding a filthy rag in one hand. "I told you not to open your eyes," she scolded.

He tried to speak, grimaced and spat out whatever

was in his mouth. More mud. He'd been lying on his side in a ditch.

In a ditch?

What the hell was he doing in a ditch?

A voice kept echoing in his head. Someone screaming, "Hit the ditch, hit the ditch!"

Oh. That ditch. Evidently he'd hit it harder than intended. They both had. A kid on a bicycle had been under him, at least he remembered that much. The boy was now huddled a few feet away, pale as wet plaster except for the mud dripping off his hair, his face, his clothes. There was no sign of the bike, but a nice tubular aluminum chair lay on its side a few yards away, along with what looked like the remains of a bombed-out flea market.

Lying on his back, he gazed up at a woman who remained featureless, either because angels couldn't be seen by mere mortals, or because he was seeing her silhouetted against the sky.

She jabbed at his head again with her rag. Wincing, he caught her arm and said, "What the devil are you trying to do? Damn it, that hurts!"

Major understatement. Various parts of his body were beginning to report in to command central. The message was pain. Agonizing, unfocused pain.

"Mom, what about the horses?" Kid's voice.

"They're fine." Angel's voice.

He wanted to hang on to both, hang on to something solid until his world settled down again. *God, don't let me throw up!*

"Is he going to be all right, Mom?"

"I hope so, hon. Here, help me prop him up."

"Do you think you can walk?" That was addressed

to him, not to Hon, in a soft contralto voice he found oddly comforting.

He felt hands on his shoulders, then one slipped under his back. Something smelled like cinnamon, which was funny, because up until then all he could smell was mud and something green and faintly resinous.

He tried to shift to a sitting position and yelped as pain stabbed his left knee all the way up to his groin.

"Don't touch him, hon. You might have to go for help."

"But, Mama, my bike's gone."

"Then go home and call nine-one-one."

"But, Mom—"

Mom the Angel sighed. "What am I thinking? The lines are probably down. I don't even know if the town's still there. Oh, God."

He wanted to tell her to use his cell phone, but the impulse died as he realized the phone was in his car and at the moment, there was no vehicle in sight. Where the hell was his car? Did he even have one?

Well, sure he had one. Why else would he be stuck out here in the middle of nowhere? He'd been on his way to—

Where? Where the hell am I going? A sense of urgency overrode the pain and he struggled to get up.

Firm hands held him down. "Wait," she said. "We don't know yet if anything's broken."

Taking the line of least resistance, he closed his eyes again, releasing the vague feeling of urgency as pain rolled over him in shuddering waves. The woman leaned over and placed her hands on his sides, patting him down as if she were searching for weapons. "I'm just trying to see if anything's noticeably out of place," she said apologetically. "I took a course in first aid a few years ago."

When she got as far as his knees, he began to curse, then bit it off. "Sorry," he muttered. "Kids and angels don't—"

"Shh, I've heard worse. Look, I didn't find anything obviously broken, but your left knee feels swollen to me. Was it that way before—" She broke off, biting her lip. "Oh, lordy, I hope I didn't do anything awful when I rolled you over onto your side. Pete was half under water. I had to pull him out from under you."

"Give me a minute," he growled. Carefully, he flexed his fingers, testing. So far, so good. Wrists still functioned, arms and elbows were still in working order. They hurt like the devil, but still obeyed his brain's instructions.

The angel said something about rocks in the ditch, as if that might explain everything. Next time he took a header he'd make certain there were no rocks in the ditch first. "I think they're just chunks of old culverts," she said apologetically. "From when they replaced them along this stretch of highway winter before last."

As if he gave a damn.

He moved his left leg and sucked air in through his teeth. Not a good sign. "Would you mind looking to see if there's a bone poking through my skin?" he said through clenched jaws.

Tearfully—he could have sworn he saw tears streaking down her face—she leaned back and peered at the lower half of his body. If he was in bad enough shape to make an angel weep, he wasn't too sure he cared to hear the details.

"I don't think it's broken, but you must have twisted it. There's part of a pine tree lying over there—lots of junk everywhere. You probably tripped. I think your left ankle might be sprained, too, but I don't think it's broken. Is that your shoe caught under that branch over there? Pete, how about digging it out?''

"Left knee, left ankle.'' His attempt at a smile was more of a grimace. "The good news is, I've still got one good limb, otherwise you'd have to shoot me.''

"Hush,'' she said sternly. "Lie still a minute and let me think.''

He didn't have a whole lot of choice. Aside from the injuries she'd mentioned, he'd already discovered a lump above his left temple that was roughly the size of a West Texas cantaloupe.

And then he lost it again. Flat out fainted. Later he had to wonder how they'd managed to get him up and moving. Angels, he figured, had their methods. He didn't remember flying. Sure as hell didn't remember any harp music. Remembered hearing a siren in the distance that wailed on and on and on until he felt like taking it out with a high-powered rifle. Somewhere a dog was barking. At least the kid had stopped whimpering. Now he couldn't seem to shut up, chattering on and on about the noise, and how scared he was, and wow, look at all those broken trees.

By the time he was able to focus on anything besides his own pain, they had reached a shabby, two-story farmhouse neatly surrounded by two-thirds of a picket fence.

Working together to support his not-inconsiderable weight, the kid and the woman, who was a lot stronger than she looked, had managed to ease him onto the front porch. Somewhere during the painful journey he'd figured out that she was no angel. He remembered gazing up from his undignified position in the foul-smelling wheelbarrow they'd used to trundle him down a long, bumpy lane, to focus on her face. It was probably not the most beautiful face he'd ever seen, but he'd clung to the image, because he'd desperately needed to cling to something.

"Give me a minute," he gasped. Seated on the porch floor, both hands gripping his swollen knee, he focused on riding over the pain. Breathe in, breathe out, slowly and deeply. Count off, count off, count off....

A glimpse of something vaguely familiar slipped in and out of his mind—a mind that admittedly wasn't working too well at the moment. Uniforms...semi-automatic weapons...?

His head felt as if it had been shot out of a mortar.

"I don't know how to thank you," the woman said.

Squinting through narrowed eyes, he sized her up when she came and knelt in front of him. She was soaking wet, dirty, but had all the right curves in all the right places. Oh, yeah—he'd have to be dead to miss that much. Green eyes, brown hair—nice, but nothing fancy. The kind of woman a man might have given a second look, but probably no more. And yet...

"Do I know you?" he asked cautiously. He felt the need to reach out and hold on to something—someone—familiar. At the same time he felt an unsettling need for caution.

Why?

Who knew?

"I don't think so. I'm Ellen Wagner. The boy you saved is my son, Pete. I'll never be able to repay you, Mr....?"

There was something at once earthy and ethereal about her. Thin face, hollow cheeks, haunting eyes— or maybe he meant haunted. Without being actually pretty, she was beautiful. She was obviously waiting for him to introduce himself. He ran a quick mental check before the walls slammed down.

It'll come, he thought with growing desperation. This kind of thing happened in books and movies, not in real life. At least, not to him.

Whoever the hell he was.

By the time he woke up again, it was pitch-dark. There was a night-light on, one of those small, fake-candle things. He waited for his eyes to adjust. Nothing looked familiar. He didn't know what he'd been expecting, but nothing about the room rang any bells. Evidently he wasn't at home. He couldn't quite remember what home looked like, but he'd lay odds this wasn't it.

Cautiously sitting up, he began to swing his legs over the side of the bed. Pain slammed through him as it all came back.

Correction. The immediate past came back. For all he knew he could've been born in a ditch with a pale-faced angel for a midwife and a skinny wet kid for an assistant.

Hell of a thing. He was used to—

What? He didn't know what he was used to; he only knew this wasn't it.

"How long have I been out of it?" he asked as the woman came silently into the bedroom. Any minute now, he assured himself, things would begin to click into place.

She was barefoot. White robe, no halo, no wings. Avid for information, he latched onto the smallest detail. She glanced at her watch. A man's watch, he noted, on a delicate wrist.

"It's just past eleven now—p.m. They say the tornado struck at seven minutes to one this afternoon. I woke you up several times just to be sure you were all right, the way you're supposed to with a head injury. Don't you remember?''

"Lady, I don't remember shi—anything.'' Evidently he did remember how to talk to a lady.

"We'll have to call you something. What comes to mind?''

"Bathroom. And no, I don't want to be called John, but if you'll point me in the right direction, I'd be much obliged.''

Seeing the smile that trembled on her lips, he'd have given anything to have met her under better circumstances.

She indicated a door across the hall and mentally he measured the distance. If he could grab a chair he could probably use it to lurch across the room.

"You really need to keep your left leg elevated as much as possible,'' she told him.

"I can handle it.'' He could handle the pain better than he could handle asking her to help with his more intimate needs.

"There was a crutch—I think I put it in the attic. If you'll wait right here a minute, I'll run see.''

"Take your time,'' he said through a clenched jaw.

Evidently she recognized his most pressing problem at the moment. She was gone and back before he could decide whether to risk falling on his face or an even worse indignity.

"Here, I don't know if it's the right height. It was in the attic when we moved in. Thank goodness I never got around to clearing things out.''

She eased into position under his arm to help him up, and even in his battered condition, he recognized the smell of a woman fresh from her bath. At any other time he had a feeling he'd have responded to it.

She handed him the crutch and helped him position it before he embarrassed himself. It was short, but at least it allowed him some mobility. He thanked her and hobbled off to tend to nature's call. And incidentally, to look in the mirror to see who the hell he was.

The face that stared back at him moments later would have looked right at home on any Wanted poster. A jaw that redefined the word stubborn. A largish nose that canted slightly to the southwest. High forehead, distorted at the moment by the large, discolored lump above his left temple. Nothing rang any bells, including the stubble, the mud-stiffened brown hair and the suspicious dark eyes. After staring for long moments at the mirror image, he felt like crying. Howling like a lovesick coyote.

If he'd ever before come face-to-face with the man in the mirror, he didn't remember it.

He managed to wash up, even doused his head in the basin a few times to remove some of the mud. The rest he left behind on one of her pretty pink towels.

She was still there when he made it back to the room. Ms. Wagner. Mrs. Wagner. She had a son.

Think, man! Get it together!

How the devil could he get it together when his head felt like a filing cabinet that had been bludgeoned with a sledgehammer? The image of a silver-gray metal filing cabinet flickered in and out so fast he didn't have time to latch on to any details.

"Are you hungry? We had supper hours ago, but I could heat you some soup. What about chicken noodle?"

"Coffee. Strong, black and sweet. I don't usually

take sugar, but I need the…'' His voice trailed off as it occurred to him that things were starting to come back. Any minute now he'd remember who he was, and where he was supposed to be. According to the boy, he'd been in a hell of a hurry, but then, with a tornado bearing down on them, that was understandable.

Was anyone looking for him? A family? A wife? Chances were that whatever transportation had brought him this far was no longer available. Picturing the scene when he'd first looked around that ditch, he didn't recall seeing anything resembling wheels. Not even the kid's bike.

"What shall I call you?" She was waiting quietly. Patience was a quality he'd always admired, especially in a woman. Without knowing how he knew, he knew.

"Uh, might as well call me Storm."

She had a way of tilting her head that spoke louder than words. *You're kidding, right?*

"Look, I seem to have temporarily mislaid a few things. Like my long-term memory. Can we just make it easy until I get it back?"

"I'll bring you the coffee, but you'd probably better eat something, too. The minute the lines are up I'll call my doctor."

"My cell phone—" He broke off, confused, frustrated—feeling helpless and somehow knowing it was not something he was accustomed to feeling.

"If you had one, it wasn't on you when I found you."

It was then he noticed for the first time that his shirt was striped cotton, and so were his drawstring pants. They were also too wide and too short.

"I never wear pajamas," he said, oddly offended.

"You do now. No matter how sick you are, you're not getting into my bed in those muddy rags you were wearing. I threw away your tie—it was hopeless. I washed your shirt and underwear. As for your pants, well, I sponged them, but I doubt if even a dry cleaner will be able to do much with them. I'm sorry. Pete went back and found your other shoe. I did the best I could, but I'm afraid they'll never be the same. Cordovan leather doesn't take kindly to being scrubbed inside and out, even with saddle soap."

He took a moment to absorb the implications. There were several. There might be something in one of his pockets that would give him a clue as to his identity— even a monogram would help. Half joking, he said, "I don't suppose you found a name, address and serial number among my effects, did you?"

"Serial number?"

Serial number? "I mean phone number. Hell, I don't know, I'm just reaching here. Help me out, will you?"

"Sorry. You were wearing a nice wristwatch, but I'm afraid it didn't survive. The crystal was broken and it was full of muddy water. You might be right about your name, though. There was a handkerchief in your hip pocket that had what looked like an H with an S in the middle—sort of a design, you know? Storm...hits? Storm Help? Harry Storm?"

"Nice try. Don't worry, it'll come. And tell your husband thanks for the use of his pajamas."

"I'm a widow," she said quietly. "I kept Jake's things after he died because...well, just because, I guess." Leaning her hips against the dresser, arms crossed over her breasts, she shrugged. "I'd better go heat some soup—I hope canned is okay. I'll bring the coffee as soon as it's made."

"I see the power's on."

"Ours wasn't off more than a few hours, but just up the road—you can see some of it from here—things are pretty torn up. A few miles south of here, two farms and a trailer park were completely wiped out. I'm not sure about the rest, I haven't had time to watch much news."

"Casualties?"

"None reported so far."

"Do you have a radio I can borrow?"

"I can bring one in, but right now you probably need sleep more than you need news. If you can make it as far as the living room in the morning, you can eat breakfast while you watch the storm coverage on TV. Maybe something will ring a bell."

She left then, and he sat for a moment longer and considered what he knew and what he didn't.

What he knew was easy. He was alive. He'd been rescued by a widow with a kid named Pete, although he was usually called Hon. Her husband, Jake, had been shorter and broader. As for the widow herself, she had a surprisingly womanly body under the baggy clothes she'd been wearing when she'd found him in that ditch and the bathrobe she'd worn later.

Oh, yeah, he knew all that, all right. It was what he didn't know that was giving him fits. Like who the devil he was.

Like where he'd been going in such a hell of a hurry. Like what he had been doing that had left this nagging sense of urgency inside him. Almost a sense of wariness.

Like what happened to his vehicle.

And which one of them—the woman or her son— had got him out of his clothes and into these striped pajamas.

Two

At a quarter to midnight, after checking the doors and switching off the outside lights, Ellen glanced toward the stairs, feeling as if she'd just run a three-day marathon. Pete was finally asleep; the stranger had been fed and was now sleeping—safely and normally, she sincerely hoped. When he'd opened his eyes earlier, she'd looked closely and could detect no sign of irregular pupils, but with such dark eyes it was hard to tell.

Nice eyes, really. It wasn't like her to notice a man's eyes—or a man's anything else. But as she'd been the one to get him out of his clothes and into a pair of pajamas…

Well, there were some things no woman who wasn't blind and totally devoid of hormones could help but notice.

She yawned. She would try to cram eight hours of sleep into what was left of the night, but she knew in advance that it wouldn't be enough. All too soon the alarm clock would go off and she'd have to get up again, get Pete off to school. After that, unless Booker and Clyde showed up, she would turn out the horses, come back inside and make the beds and put the breakfast dishes in to soak, then go back to the barn and muck out the stalls, clean troughs and do all the other things she paid that worthless pair to do. Even when they went through the motions, she had to follow right behind them to see that things were done properly. It was almost easier to do them herself in the first place, but there were still some jobs that needed a man's strength.

Absently she picked up a plastic robot and a model airplane and put them on the stairs to go up. Crossing to the fireplace, she wound the mantel clock, touched the framed picture beside it and yawned again.

Lord, she was tired. There weren't enough hours in the day to accomplish all that needed doing, nor enough energy to last, even if she could have found the hours.

She was halfway up the stairs when someone knocked on the front door. "Oh, shoot, what now?" she muttered, glancing at her watch. No matter how tired she was, she could hardly ignore a summons in the middle of the night, not after what had happened only a few hours ago. She'd got off lucky. Others hadn't been so fortunate. If someone needed her help...

She switched on the security light again and peered out the window. A dark car had pulled up to the front gate, one of those low-slung models with a spoiler on the rear end and decorations all over the body. Long, curling flames, in this case.

Almost everyone she knew drove a truck, but most families also had a car. That detailing, though, was unfamiliar.

"May I help you?" She opened the door only a few inches, keeping her right foot wedged against the bottom so that she could slam it shut if need be. If worse came to worst, Jake's old .420 gauge shotgun was propped in the corner behind the coatrack. Of course the shells were upstairs in her dresser under her socks and sweaters, but a housebreaker wouldn't know that.

House-breakers also didn't go around knocking on front doors.

"Yes'm, that is, we're looking for a friend of ours. He ain't been seen since them twisters went through here, and we thought he might've run into some trouble."

If she'd had antennae, they would definitely have been twitching. Not that she had anything in particular against tattoos—it was purely a matter of personal preference—but this man was covered with them. "A friend, you say?"

"Oh, yes, ma'am, he's a real good friend. We been on his tail since—" His silent companion elbowed him, and he stepped back and cleared his throat. "That is, we sure would like to find him, ma'am. You seen any strangers passing through here since the twister cut through?"

Later, Ellen would wonder what on earth had possessed her to lie. It wasn't her nature at all, but something about this pair set off alarms. She put it down to a cross between a woman's intuition and a mother's protective instincts. "Only the men from the power company. They were checking all along here. One of them came by earlier today to be sure my power was back on."

"Power company, huh? You sure you haven't seen nobody else?"

"Perhaps if you described your friend?"

"'Bout six feet tall, maybe a few inches taller, wouldn't you say?" He looked at his companion, who nodded vigorously. "Dark hair, dark eyes—I guess if I was a lady, I might call him good-looking." His mouth stretched into a smile that didn't reach his eyes. They remained flat and expressionless.

"What's your friend's name?"

The two men looked at each other. It was the tattooed man who spoke. "Harrison. J. S. Harrison. Ma'am."

Ellen tucked the name away to consider later. "And your names?"

A furtive look passed between the two men. "I'm Bill Smith and this here is, uh, Bill Jones."

Right, Ellen thought. And I'm the president's mother-in-law. She wouldn't trust either one of these men to take out her garbage. "I'm sorry, I can't help you, but if I see anyone fitting that description, I'll be sure to tell him you're looking for him."

The devil she would. The moment she closed the door and shot the bolt, she moved to the window to make sure they left. For several minutes they stood outside their car, heads close together as if they were talking. What if she'd been wrong and they really were friends of her stranger?

J. S. Harrison. That at least sounded plausible. What kind of man was she harboring under her roof? If he was a friend of Smith and Jones, she didn't want him anywhere on her property.

Finally they got into the car, made a three-point turn and headed back down the lane. At the rate they were driving, if their muffler survived the potholes, she'd be very much surprised. She told herself she was being paranoid, but then, just down the hall, a stranger was sleeping in Jake's bed. A man she didn't know from Adam.

A man who didn't know himself from Adam. Maybe she should have let them in to meet him—at least they might have told him who he was and where he belonged.

And maybe not, she thought, stroking away the goose bumps that suddenly pricked her upper arms.

On impulse, she slipped quietly into the downstairs bedroom and gazed at the sleeping stranger. Who are you? she wondered. Have I just made a serious blunder? Were those two men really your friends?

She didn't think so. His name might actually be Harrison. Then again, there was no J. in his monogram.

Ellen would be the first to admit that she could be wrong about this whole business. The description they'd given her could fit half the men in Lone Star County. Six feet tall, lean but powerful build, dark hair and eyes. They hadn't mentioned the shape of his mouth or the way his eyebrows lifted at the inner ends when he was puzzled, but then, men probably wouldn't even notice such things.

Still, she might have solved all his problems if she'd let them come in and look. Some of his problems, anyway. It certainly wouldn't have hurt...would it?

That was the trouble, she just didn't know. She did know this man had been injured saving her son's life. She owed him more than she could ever repay, and if that meant lying on his behalf, then she would lie until her tongue blistered.

She'd have to tell him about the men, of course, as soon as his knot went down and his headache eased. It would help if she could come up with some logical reason for her reaction. A woman's intuition? She could just hear him jeering at that. Men always did.

"You sent them away? Because you didn't like their looks? Are you crazy, or what?"

Okay, so she was crazy. She'd done what she thought best at the time. It wasn't the first time she'd ever acted on impulse. If that made her guilty of some crime, so be it. At the moment her guest was her responsibility. In his vulnerable state he was in no condition to defend himself against a couple of weirdos who came knocking on her door in the middle of the night.

"So sue me," she muttered, collecting the supper tray on her way out.

The man called Storm struggled to absorb and process information, but it was slow going. One thing he knew—his head still hurt like hell. And he knew he wasn't about to take any painkillers, not without knowing more about himself than he did. He'd heard of people taking a simple over-the-counter remedy and going into shock.

He'd heard of it? Where? Who?

"Think, man, think!"

The trouble was, whenever he tried to reach out mentally and latch on to something solid—some glimmer of information hiding just beneath the surface of his mind—it slipped away. He didn't have time to waste sleeping. He needed to stay awake long enough to put two and two together and come up with some answers, but he kept dozing off.

It was still pitch-black outside. He seemed to recall being awakened several times. Gingerly feeling the knot on the side of his head, he winced.

Head wound. Concussion. Check the pupils.

He knew that much, at least. Maybe he was a medic, a doctor.

The woman—Ellen Wagner—had been frantic over her son. "I knew he was on his way home from Joey's," she'd said. "But when I saw that sky…"

She'd taken several deep breaths then, unable to go

on. Oddly enough, he understood how she'd felt. There was a hell of a lot he didn't understand yet, but that much, he did. She was a mother. Her kid had been threatened; she'd reacted. She was still reacting.

So what did that mean—that he had a mother or that he had a son?

The boy was sound asleep, she'd told him the last time she'd roused him to be sure he was still alive. Or maybe the time before that—he'd lost all sense of time. She should have gone to bed hours ago, but she'd stayed up to wake him periodically in case he started showing signs of a concussion. Sometime during the night she'd taken the trouble to heat a can of chicken noodle soup, telling him that her son used to call it chicken oogle soup. The small confidence hadn't triggered any buried memories, but the soup had helped stave off the shakes.

He knew now that he was in a downstairs bedroom she'd furnished for her husband after he'd grown too weak to climb the stairs. She'd told him that when he asked. He might not know who he was, but at least he knew where he was. In a pine-paneled room on a small ranch about five miles from the town of Mission Creek, in Lone Star County, in the State of Texas.

That part felt right, anyway. The Texas part. It didn't really ring any bells—he could have been from the planet Pluto for all he knew—but somehow, Texas felt right.

It was just beginning to get light outside when she came to bring him her late husband's shaving kit. "I thought shaving might make you feel better. I'm not sure about letting you stand long enough to take a shower, though. If you got dizzy and fell…"

"Maybe you could roll me outside and hose me down."

She was obviously running on fumes. He wondered how much sleep she'd gotten during the night. Judging from the early hour, it couldn't have been much.

She took the time to give him a general description of the area. "It's mostly small farms and cattle ranches. We have year round grazing here, so cattle are a big thing, but crops are big, too. At this point our farm hardly qualifies as a working ranch—we're just hanging on to status quo, you might say, but— Oh, I don't know why I even said that, you couldn't possibly be interested. Anyway, we love it here. It's a great place to raise a son."

If she was hoping something she said would trigger his memory, she was disappointed. They both were. She had a nice voice, though. A bit raspy, as if she might have screamed herself hoarse searching for the boy. She'd be the type, he was somehow sure of it, to run outside in the teeth of a tornado to rescue her child.

Lucky kid.

During the wakeful periods of the night they'd exchanged a few words—just enough to let her know he hadn't gone off the deep end. From a few things she'd said, he'd gained the impression that she and the boy might be having a pretty rough time keeping their heads above water. Not that she'd complained. He'd had to ask a few leading questions. Somewhat surprisingly, he'd discovered that he was good at it, even when he wasn't particularly interested in the answers.

Although, oddly enough, he was. The woman was nothing to him. He'd brushed off her gratitude, saying that whatever he'd done for her son, she had more than returned the favor by hauling his ass out of that ditch.

Not that he'd phrased it that way. Which told him something else about himself. It wasn't enough, but it was a beginning.

Some five miles away, a terse conversation was taking place between two men. The air was redolent with the smoke of a Cuban cigar. "I'm telling you, Frank, he's dead. He's gotta be dead, else them two guys I sent scouting around woulda found him. They found what was left of his car over by that Quik-Fill place out on 59. I had 'em haul it to the chopshop."

"You're sure it was Harrison's?"

"I had a guy run the plates. 'Sides, his coat was still inside caught up in some branches where a tree limb busted through the windshield. Big mama! Rammed clean through the front and out the back. Man, nobody coulda lived through that! Hood's gone, one o' the doors ripped off. Nothing left but scrap metal."

Lying on a polished table between the two men was a sodden wallet, a driver's license, several credit cards, a Triple-A membership card and ninety-eight dollars in cash. No one had reported the missing credit cards.

"Where the hell is he?" the older man muttered, stabbing his cigar at the driver's license issued to one J. Spencer Harrison, six feet, one inch tall, one hundred eighty-seven pounds, brown hair, brown eyes, born November 4, 1967.

"Man, I'm telling you, nobody could've survived that hit. Ask me, he's buzzard bait by now."

Frank Del Brio paced in a tight circle, occasionally thumping ashes onto the plush carpet. After several minutes of silence he turned and jabbed his stub of a cigar toward the other man. "You ask around?"

"You know me, Frank. I say I'll check something out, I check it out."

"Who'd you send?"

"Sal and Peaches."

"Jesus Christ, man, those two couldn't find their ass with a road map!"

"You wanted it kept quiet, didn't you? Sal don't talk and Peaches owes me."

More pacing. More scattered ashes. Finally, as if he'd come to a conclusion, Del Brio turned to face his companion. "I'm gonna have to trust you on this one. Joe Ed's already positioned to take his place, but I swear to you, if Harrison turns up once a new D. A. is appointed, there's no place south of the North Pole I can't find you. You might want to notify your next of kin, just in case."

Ellen roused Pete and got him ready for school. They probably wouldn't get much work done today, as everyone would be full of talk about the tornado. She tried not to think about the two men who had showed up only hours earlier. If they'd been telling the truth about a dear friend who'd been missing since yesterday, wouldn't they have seemed more upset? More concerned? Not that they hadn't tried, but they hadn't been convincing. Something about the whole scene had struck her as off-key, and she was a firm believer in instinct. Jake used to tease her about relying on what he called her witch's antenna, but even he had eventually learned to listen to her.

Only by then, it had been too late.

When she'd looked out and seen those two men at her front door, every ounce of intuition she possessed had warned her against revealing the presence of her stranger. Once his memory returned she would tell him and let him make the decision. They were certainly easy enough to describe. If "Smith" and "Jones" were such good friends of his, he would know how to reach them. It would be his decision to make, not hers.

By the time she came in to collect his tray after getting Pete off to school and letting the horses into the paddock, he'd fallen asleep again. For several moments she stood silently at the foot of the bed and gazed down at him. How many hours had she sat beside that same bed, in this same room, watching Jake sleep, telling herself that at least when he was sleeping, he wasn't in actual pain. Praying that that was true....

Evidently Storm had used the shaving things. Awake, he'd looked older. Even wary. Asleep, he looked oddly vulnerable. His features were too irregular to be called handsome, yet he was strikingly attractive, even with a purple lump on the side of his head. "Whoever you are," she murmured, "you're safe here." It was the best she could do in return for his saving Pete's life.

The next time he awoke he would probably remember who he was and call someone to come for him if they couldn't locate his car. If he had any sense at all, he'd have them drive him directly to the hospital in Mission Creek for X rays.

Once he was gone things would go back to the way they'd been before, with her and Pete and two no-account hired hands trying to do the work she and Jake and Mr. Caster had done before her world had fallen apart.

Ellen's shoulders drooped. She was tired before the day even started. Booker and Clyde, the two transients she'd recently hired, were no more than adequate even when they were sober. They didn't know nearly as much about horses as they'd claimed when they'd showed up looking for work, but at least they were willing to work for what she could afford to pay and weren't too proud to take orders from a woman. Desperate to hang on to what they had without having to turn to her father again—something she had sworn she would never do—she had hired them on the spot.

After washing off a scratch, she dabbed on antiseptic, winced at the sharp sting and sighed. Sometimes she wished she could just take a single day off and do something frivolous, such as curl up with a good book and read and sleep all day long, or take Pete to a circus, or even a movie in town.

Christmas was only a few weeks away, and she hadn't even thought of what she was going to get him. A bike, of course, but some little surprise would be nice.

With no heritage of his own, Jake had been determined to build one for their son. Now Jake was gone, but with any luck, she'd be able to raise their son right here, the way they had planned. Pete would grow up on Wagner property. Eventually he would marry and have children of his own, and one day, if they were lucky, her grandchildren would grow up here along with the descendants of the quarter horses she and Jake had bought with such high hopes for the future.

She'd made meat loaf and mashed potatoes for supper last night and served leftovers for lunch. Her mystery man had eaten little either time, and talked even less. Fine. He needed rest more than anything else, and she was too tired to make conversation.

Funny, the way a dream could change, she mused as she washed the supper dishes. One dream simply merged into another, and then another as time went on, evolving, but never quite losing the essential core.

The only dream she had room for now was to guide her son safely through the next few years to try to make up for his lack of a father. It wouldn't be long until she'd be dealing with an adolescent instead of a sweet child who was almost too eager to please—almost as if he were afraid she would go away, too, the way his father had.

She had done everything she could think of to reassure him—they had talked to a counselor at the school. But Ellen knew that she alone was responsible for raising her son to be a decent, responsible adult. She didn't know how much of a role model she could be, but she fully intended to give it her best shot. They would make it. One way or another, she would see to it.

"And as for you, my mysterious stranger," she whispered, "I'll take care of you, too, for as long as you need me. I owe you."

He was still sleeping when she glanced in again before heading upstairs to her own bed. This time she didn't try to rouse him. It had been more than twenty-four hours now and there'd been no indication of a concussion. And he really did need his sleep. The sooner he healed and remembered, the sooner he'd be off her hands and the sooner she could get back to building Pete a legacy from a few horses and a few hundred acres.

After pulling the light quilt up over his shoulders, she felt his forehead with the back of her hand, then tiptoed from the room, leaving the door ajar in case he needed anything. It was almost like having two sons to care for.

Oh, no, it wasn't. She didn't know what she felt toward the man called Storm, other than gratitude, but whatever it was, it wasn't even faintly maternal. No way!

He would probably insist on getting out of bed tomorrow. Men could be stubborn about such things, taking any kind of sickness or injury as a threat to their manhood. Jake had been the same way. He wouldn't admit to having allergies even when he was sneezing his head off, his nose running and his eyes all watery. As if hay fever somehow negated his masculinity.

Oh, Jake, she thought, sighing. She had long since run out of tears, but she still wept inside her heart. After more than two years she still caught herself glancing around, expecting to see him kicking the mud off his boots on the back porch, or hanging over the paddock fence, gloating over his precious horses. Two yearling mares, two geldings and a stallion. Hardly the mix he'd been planning on, but he'd bought the lot of them at a bargain price from a man who'd unexpectedly been forced to relocate.

They had mapped it all out on paper—the buying, the breeding strategy, but they'd hardly got started when Jake had been diagnosed with a particularly virulent and fast-growing form of cancer. He had died just thirteen months after they had bought the ranch and moved to Lone Star County.

And dear God, a part of her had died with him. If it hadn't been for Pete, she didn't know what she would have done. Going back home had never been an option. She didn't know what her own father would have thought of his grandson if they ever met, but that wasn't going to happen. Never again would she beg. Leonard Summerlin had disowned her when she'd married against his will and turned his back when she had needed his help so desperately.

Not for the first time, the irony of the situation struck her. Unless he fathered a son of his own, Pete was her father's sole male descendent. For a man who liked to think of himself as a dynasty builder, Leonard Summerlin was his own worst enemy.

He had told her countless times that she was just like her mother, then gone on to recount her mother's shortcomings. Celinda Summerlin was vain—but then, Celinda Summerlin had been beautiful. Ellen had never had anything to be vain about. According to her father, Celinda hadn't a clue when it came to managing money, but even as a child Ellen had understood that her mother had never had enough money to manage before marrying Leonard Summerlin.

When it came to managing, Ellen had been no better, no worse than most of her friends at staying within her allowance. In later years she had discovered somewhat surprisingly that the less there was to manage, the better a manager she became. The bank in Mission Creek that held the mortgage on the ranch had advised her to lease out most of her acreage, keeping back only enough for pasturage and to grow feed for the horses. That way, the banker had explained, she could be certain of meeting the mortgage payments with a bit left over without the risk of losing an entire crop to flood, drought or a sudden freeze. The weather everywhere, he'd reminded her, had been increasingly erratic over the past few years.

It had seemed sensible to her. She had kept the stock although she hadn't known the first thing about horses, much less about breeding them. But the horses had been Jake's dream, and she was determined to hang on to as much of that dream as she could for their son. She might have come from a privileged background, but from someone—her mother, most likely—she had inherited a backbone. Dust-bowl-survivor genes, Jake had called it, teasing her about the way her jaw squared off when she got what he'd called her I-shall-not-be-moved look on her face.

Whatever it was, grit or survivor genes, it had enabled her to get through another day and then another one when she couldn't see her way through the coming night, much less the years ahead.

"No way," the man called Storm said adamantly. "Look, I'll get out of your hair if my being here is a problem, but I'm not going to any damned hospital for a simple sprain and a headache."

"Oh, hush up and let me think," Ellen grumbled. They'd been arguing about how long it had been. She'd said this made three days. The man had said he could only remember one, and not too much of that.

Pete grinned. He'd come in to bring the morning paper just as his mother was fussing at him again. Boy, it sure was cool to hear her fussing at a grown man the same way she did him when he wouldn't finish his macaroni and cheese or forgot to put his dirty clothes in the hamper.

"All right," his mama said finally, laying down the law. He knew that tone. Man, did he ever! "You can get out of bed and come in the living room. I know you're dying to watch the storm coverage on TV, but you're going to keep that foot up and if I hear one more peep out of you about leaving, I'm going to—"

Pete watched, grinning broadly.

The man watched. He was scowling.

"—to call the paramedics to come haul you off and you can argue with them for a change. I just don't see what's so awful about having a doctor look you over. For all you know, you might have some broken bones. There are hundreds of bones in your feet, and your foot's not all that far from your ankle."

Storm looked at Pete and lifted a brow. "She go on like this a lot?"

Solemnly the boy nodded. "Yessir, that she does, but she means well. That's what my daddy always said."

Ellen's hands flew up in a gesture of surrender. "All right, be one, then!"

"That's what she always says," Pete confided. "Daddy used to tell her B1 was a bomber, and she'd just walk off the way she's doing now, all huffy and puffy. She's not really mad, though."

Storm didn't think she was, either. Somewhere among the jumbled miscellaneous impressions he'd dredged up was the knowledge that women acted that way when they cared about someone who refused to bow to their superior wisdom.

How the hell do I know that? Do I have a wife? Daughters?

Irritated, frustrated and amused, he said, "Your mother says you're a checkers champ. Lay out the board, son. Best two out of three, okay?"

"You bet! But first I'd better go feed up and fill the trough. Booker and Clyde, they're pro'ly drunk again. Don't tell Ma, though. She threatened to fire 'em next time she caught 'em drinking."

"Sounds like a pretty good idea to me."

They continued the conversation after the boy completed his chores. While Pete got out the checkerboard, Storm reiterated his suggestion. From what he'd heard about the two hired hands, they weren't the type any decent man would want around his wife and child.

"Know what? They smoke, too. My mom said if she ever caught 'em smoking in the barn around all that hay and stuff, she'd run 'em off with a pitchfork."

"Smart woman, your mama."

Pete shrugged his skinny shoulders. Emptying out the worn drawstring bag, he began setting up the board. Without looking up, he said, "Know what? Booker's cigarettes don't smell much like Mr. Ludlum's. They smell more like a chicken house. They look kind of funny, too."

Very carefully, Storm centered a black checker in a red square. He was going on sheer instinct. "They ever offer you a smoke?"

"Nope. I wouldn't take it if they did. I promised Mom."

Storm made a tentative move, which Pete promptly countered. He had an idea there was more being handed around in that barn than a bottle of hooch and a filter tip. Frowning, he made another move.

Pete promptly jumped his man and glanced up, a triumphant grin lighting his bony little face. "Gotcha!"

"Fair and square. I'd better concentrate on what I'm doing here. I didn't figure you to be this good."

"I'm pretty good, all right. I beat Mom almost every game, but that's pro'ly 'cause she lets me."

"I wouldn't be too sure."

Storm hadn't even been sure when he'd offered to play whether he knew how. Evidently, he did. They played in silence for a few more minutes. Then, without looking up, the boy said, ''Trouble is, if Mom gets rid of Clyde and Booker, we'll have to do everything ourselves again, and she's no good at pulling wire. Last time we tried to fix a section of fence she couldn't hardly get out of bed the next day. She's even worse with a post-hole digger than she is with a wire puller, but I'm not tall enough yet. We had us an auger for the tractor, but the P.T.O. got broke.''

''The what?''

Frowning, Pete tried to describe, using his hands, how the power take-off worked with different attachments. ''I get the idea,'' Storm said. And he did—sort of. ''What about your neighbors? Can't one of them lend you a couple of hands for certain jobs?''

''Nobody wants to work for a woman.'' It was a simple declarative statement. Pete looked up from the checkerboard, disgust clear on his tanned face. ''Sides, we're already scraping the bottom of the barrel. Least, that's what my friend Joey's pa says. Mr. Ludlum says men don't like taking orders from a woman, even when she's the boss.'' He shrugged his bony shoulders and clapped a crown on one of the reds. ''My mom's real smart, but Booker, he calls her stuff behind her back.'' The boy's face turned a dusky red as he concentrated on the worn checkers.

Storm felt something inside him tighten like a fist. One thing he would do before he left—have a talk with this Booker fellow, whoever and whatever he was. Anger crammed in on the frustration he felt at being laid up, both mentally and physically. He had a strong feeling he wasn't used to inaction. Restlessness didn't begin to describe his reaction. Wariness came closer.

What the devil did he have to be wary about? Was he an escaped prisoner? A drug runner? They weren't all that far from the border. Then, too, there was something about the state prison....

It was gone. The impression flickered through his mind like a firefly, then winked out before he could catch it.

"Gotcha! Mr. Storm, I gotta go help Mom bring in the horses and rub 'em down now. Booker and Clyde, they've got to unload the hay wagon 'cause I can't lift the bales yet."

"Yeah, you go ahead, son. We'll play more later—after you've done your homework."

Mr. Storm. The name wasn't a perfect fit, but it felt pretty close.

The next day went largely like the others. Storm was increasingly aware of the creeping hours and increasingly fed up with being out of commission. His head still ached, but it was a manageable ache—nothing he couldn't handle. Disdaining the use of the crutch, he limped into the living room and plopped down on the sofa. His knee still suffered the occasional twinge if he turned too quickly, but most of the swelling was gone. His ankle was better, too, as long as he didn't overdo it.

He was damned tired, though, of having to wear another man's clothes. The sooner he got back to his own home, his own clothes and his own business—wherever and whatever that was—the better he'd like it. Hadn't anyone even reported him missing? A business partner, or a family member?

No man is an island. Had someone actually said that or had he only dreamed it up? Was it some great philosophical insight or gibberish? It was the damnable uncertainty that was driving him nuts. Why wasn't any-

one out searching for him? It hadn't been that long; it
only seemed that way. Was there a wife somewhere
going quietly out of her mind with worry? He didn't
feel married—however that was supposed to feel.
There was no sign that he'd ever worn a wedding ring.

Ellen wore a plain gold band. Her hands were rough,
but nicely shaped. He had a feeling his wife—if he had
one—would have smooth, pale hands with polished
nails and a full complement of jewelry.

Now why would he think that? Actually, now that
he considered it, Ellen's hands were just right for a
woman. Strong, capable, without being any less feminine. Which pretty well summed up the woman herself.

From the TV coverage he'd seen, the rash of tor-
nadoes that had barreled across the southwest corner of
Texas before streaking up the Mississippi Valley had
managed to miss the most heavily populated areas.
Thank God for that, at least. The southeast portion of
Lone Star County had suffered most of the damage.

Lone Star County. That definitely triggered a reaction, but for all he knew, he could have seen it on a
road sign. He could've been just passing through on
his way from—

From where? To where?

He swore softly and discovered that he was good at
it. Came naturally. What else, he wondered, would
come naturally? Talking to a kid? Yeah, that was no
big strain.

Talking to a woman? Touching a woman?

Again it was Ellen Wagner he thought of—the image
of her pale green eyes and tanned, hollow-cheeked
face. He thought about the woman—about the soft,
firm way she had of speaking to her son. The soft, firm

way she had touched his brow that first night when she'd thought he was sleeping.

Back off, man. You've already got more than a full caseload of trouble.

There was a framed crayon drawing hanging on the wall over the bookcase. Crudely drawn horses standing in a lime-green pasture while seven fighter jets flew overhead. Pete's signature was as big as the horses.

Oddly touched, he wondered if his own mother had ever hung one of his drawings in such a prominent place. Could he even draw? Did he have a mother?

Come on, folks, get on the ball! If I mean anything to anyone, come find me. Hide and seek gets pretty frustrating after the first few days.

Using the remote, he turned the TV on and switched channels until he found the CNN headline news. OPEC, Congress, Bosnia were in the news again.

Again? Shrugging, he switched channels, caught a name—Mercado—and swore as they went to commercial.

Mercado. Did the name mean anything, or was he grasping at straws? "Storm Mercado." He spoke out aloud, trying it on for size. It didn't fit. He muted the TV sound and reached for the newspaper. The more he scanned, the more his gut twisted. Several names snagged momentarily, but nothing came into sharp focus. Finally, in sheer desperation, he turned to the sports page.

Hell, he didn't even know who—or what—to look for there. Was he a football fan? If so, which team?

A headline read Golf Pro At Lone Star Country Club Claims Vandalism.

Lone Star Country Club. "Come on, come on," he

muttered. It was there, just beyond his reach. Like a voyeur standing outside the fall of light, watching from the darkness, he tried to see into his own mind.

And felt like crying when he failed.

Three

Thank God for Saturdays. Leaving Pete to finish up in the horse barn, Ellen came in at noon to start setting out sandwich makings for lunch. She sliced a tomato and reached for a sweet Texas onion, working with short, jerky movements.

Clyde had showed up for work about ten, smelling like a brewery. Booker hadn't made it in at all. Clyde said he had a headache.

"You mean a hangover," she'd retorted. "That's no excuse not to show up for work. I was counting on you two to repair that section of fence today."

"Tell the truth, ma'am, he weren't feelin' no pain a'tall last time I seen him." Clyde had smirked at her. He did that a lot, and it invariably drove her up a wall, but what could she do? She had to have someone. With Pete in school five days a week, she simply couldn't keep up alone.

"Hi, Mom, where's Storm?" Pete banged in through the kitchen door, stepped back, kicked off his boots, then reentered, smelling of sunshine, horses and little boy.

"Watching the noon news. I piled up pillows on the couch so he could keep his leg elevated and—"

Both turned at the sound that came from across the hall. A thud and a muffled moan. "Oh, Lord, what now?" Ellen muttered. Drying her hands on her shirt-tail, she hurried into the living room, colliding with Pete in the doorway.

Storm was on the floor, blinking awake. "What happened?" she cried, rushing to kneel beside him. "Did you hurt yourself?"

"No, this is my idea of a good time," he said, his voice like crushed gravel. "I fell asleep and rolled off the damned couch!" Pete squatted beside him and he closed his eyes. "Sorry, son. Forget I said that."

Pete, with one hand under the man's arm and the other reaching for the crutch, said solemnly, "I know stuff lots worse than damn. You ought to hear what Booker calls that old Zeus! He calls him—"

"Never mind," Ellen said repressively.

Together they managed to get him on his feet again, and Ellen suggested he move into the kitchen, as it was time for lunch. "I can pull up a stool so that you can sit and prop your foot on it."

"I don't need the stool, but thanks," he said. They'd argued about it before. She made suggestions that he ignored for the most part, but he invariably apologized for putting her to so much extra work.

Ellen didn't mind the extra effort, she really didn't. It was nice having another adult in the house. Pete seemed to enjoy him, as well.

He hobbled into the kitchen just as the back door opened and a scruffy-looking individual wearing ragged jeans and a dirty shirt came in. "This is Clyde," Ellen said, tight-lipped. "Clyde, this is Mr. Storm. Clyde, you might want to wash up." She looked pointedly at his grimy hands, then busied herself pouring iced tea, leaving the decision up to him.

"Yes'm," he said, disappearing into the washroom off the kitchen, where he stayed for all of five seconds.

"Don't think I seen you around these parts before," the hired hand said with a smirk, looking from Storm to Ellen and back.

Pete said gruffly, "Storm's visiting."

"That so?" Clyde had tracked mud into the kitchen, which Ellen made a point of sweeping up. "Sorry 'bout that, ma'am," he said, leering at Ellen's backside as she leaned into the cleaning closet to hang up the dustpan.

Storm's eyes met Pete's. The boy was furious and embarrassed, but being a boy, there wasn't a whole lot he could do about it. Storm might be impaired in a lot of ways, but that much he picked up on easily.

"This looks mighty good," he said with a smile that was patently false. *Change the subject. You're in no shape to take on the bastard in hand-to-hand, much less to take his place if he quits.*

But he was getting there. One more day and she wouldn't have to depend on that pair. Even with a sore head and a bum leg, he could shovel manure and push a wheelbarrow.

"I haven't had time to shop for groceries this week," Ellen apologized. "I heard part of the roof was torn off the warehouse next to the IGA."

"And the church steeple," Pete said with boyish excitement. "Man, it was busted to pieces! Joey said they found the pointy part way over by Mrs. Williams's house."

They made sandwiches from the ingredients she'd set out and drank iced tea and talked about the storm damage, reports of which were still coming in. Clyde didn't have much to say, but he made the little he did say unpleasant by taking a big bite of bologna, onion and cheese on white bread and talking while he chewed. As far as Storm was concerned, that alone was a firing offense.

"Man, that sure is a ugly knot on your head," Clyde said admiringly.

Storm wondered what he was supposed to say—thank you? If he'd been Pete's age, he might have said, "That sure is an ugly knot on your shoulders. What is it, your head?"

Irritated, he excused himself and stood, picking up his plate and glass. Ellen frowned at him, and he got the message. He wanted to say, "I'm not totally helpless. Let me at least do this much."

But with both Pete and Clyde watching, he remained silent. Before he left he was going to have to find a way to repay her for hauling him out of that ditch, feeding him, giving him a bed, not to mention binding up his knee and ankle and doctoring his assorted minor scrapes. Even in the shape he'd been at the time, the feel of her cool hands on his hot, swollen flesh had damn near finished him off. Under the circumstances, his reaction had been just plain crazy.

She'd even washed his shirt, his shoes and his underwear. Silk underwear. What kind of man wore silk underwear? What was he, anyway, some kind of freaking Hollywood type? A drug lord?

No way. He might not know who he was, but he sure as hell knew who he wasn't.

At the moment he was wearing a pair of her late husband's jeans, which were a few inches too short in length and slightly too big at the waist. Instead of bunching them up with a belt, he'd let them ride low on his hips. Pete said he looked cool.

Cool or not, it was the best he could do for now. His own pants were beyond help. He'd looked them over, hoping for a clue—hoping for something to jar his mind loose. A tailor's label—anything.

There'd been nothing. Nothing other than the fact that they were flawlessly tailored of an excellent worsted, cut to hang just the way a pair of pants should hang, although just how the devil he knew that, he couldn't have said.

"Do you always invite your hired hands to eat in the house with you and Pete?" he asked Ellen when they were alone together in the kitchen. Ellen had stayed behind to wash the dishes. He put away the mustard and mayonnaise and opened cabinets until he found where the salt and pepper belonged.

For a moment he thought she wasn't going to answer, but then she shrugged. "The last man did. Mr. Caster was a thoroughly decent man. Pete liked him a lot. When we bought the place, the old bunkhouse had already been turned into storage, but we were planning to clean it out and add a bathroom so he wouldn't have to commute. We never got around to it."

She didn't have to explain. There hadn't been enough time then, and there wasn't enough money now. He was getting pretty good at sizing up situations from insufficient evidence, or maybe he'd always been good at it. There was no way of knowing...yet.

"Booker and Clyde have only been working here a few weeks. Mr. Caster left toward the end of September, as soon as his social security kicked in. His arthritis was getting pretty bad, not that he'd admit it. I started advertising for a replacement as soon as he gave notice, but it didn't take long to discover that anyone even marginally competent was already working. By the time that pair of...of—"

"Bums," Storm supplied.

"To put it delicately." She spared him a fleeting smile. "Anyway, by the time they showed up, I was at my wit's end. I'm embarrassed to say I didn't even bother to check their references."

She was an easy mark, he concluded. She'd proved that much by dragging home a man she had never before laid eyes on. A vulnerable woman, living alone with her son, yet she had brought him into her home, taken care of him—even lent him her late husband's clothes and shaving gear. He could've been a proverbial ax murderer for all she knew. There were no rules that said ax murderers couldn't get caught in a tornado.

"You should have called nine-one-one and let someone else drag me out of that ditch."

She shrugged. He decided on the spot that the least he could do in return was to see that those two scoundrels who were supposed to be working for her didn't take advantage of her. The kid was willing, but at eight years old, he simply wasn't up to the task. "Ellen, a woman needs to be careful about the kinds of people she brings home with her, especially when there's a kid involved."

She looked at him, started to speak, and then bit her lip. It occurred to him that green eyes could look both clear as glass and opaque as moss, depending on the light. Or perhaps on the lady's mood.

"If you'll excuse me, I need to go turn Zeus into the large pasture. The grass there isn't nearly as good, but he gets restless in the small pen."

When the going gets uncomfortable, the uncomfortable get going. The words came to him, a paraphrase of something or other. Apt, though, he mused. "Sure, go ahead. You need some help?"

"No thanks. If you're smart, you'll get off that leg."

Whether he was smart remained to be seen. He was tempted to follow her just to prove he wasn't totally useless. He could open and shut gates, if nothing else. However, knowing that the best way to help was to stay out of the way, he spent several minutes scraping together the scant evidence he had and trying to weave it into something more solid.

Judging from the look of his hands—not to mention his clothes—he was probably a white-collar worker of some sort. Banker, broker... "Doctor, lawyer, Indian chief," he finished out loud. The situation might even have been amusing if only it weren't so damned frustrating. Just because his nails had been relatively clean when he'd been found and dragged here to the Wagner ranch, that didn't mean he was a respectable businessman. He could just as easily be a professional gambler, an embezzler, a pimp—the possibilities were endless.

And endlessly chilling.

"Think, man—concentrate! Speech patterns. Words, images—they don't come out of a vacuum."

Judging from certain speech patterns and word images that seemed to come naturally to him, while he might not be a crook, he was no stranger to the criminal life. Best case scenario, he was a cop.

A cop who wore hand-tailored suits, silk underwear and a high-dollar wristwatch? If he was a cop, then odds were better than even he was a cop on the take. The implications of that were dizzying, if not downright sickening.

Day four. That was how he counted time now. With both his past and his future a blank wall, all he could do was live in the moment and wait for an opening. One thing he'd discovered right off—patience was not his long suit. Any man, under the circumstances, would be impatient, he told himself, but rationalizing didn't help. Ellen had called him the quintessential Alpha male. He wasn't sure what she'd meant, or how she could tell, but if it meant he didn't like sitting around doing nothing more productive than sweeping, dusting and making beds—chores she'd only grudgingly allowed him to take over yesterday—then she was dead on target.

She had offered several times to go into town to ask around, to see if anyone was missing a stray male of the human species. Even offered to place an ad in the paper advertising his whereabouts. They had actually laughed over the possible wording of such an ad.

"Where would you list me, with the lost pets?" he'd asked.

"Why not? Good-tempered, house broken—we'd have to guess as to whether or not you're up to date on your shots."

He had found himself enjoying the repartee, drawn deeper by the hint of laughter that tugged at the corners of her mouth. In the kitchen doorway they'd stood toe-to-toe, eye-to-eye, caught in an extemporaneous sparring match, each daring the other to give in. It was a crazy confrontation about nothing at all, fueled by the unexpected, not to mention inappropriate way he was beginning to react to her presence. Even over such a trivial matter as a classified ad, he'd felt the adrenaline race through his body, tightening nerves, heightening senses. His own brown eyes had bored into her changeable green ones as if searching for a hint of weakness.

When it came to strengths and weaknesses, there was no contest. He'd managed to pass it off as teasing, as a joke. But for a minute there, it had felt like something entirely different.

Logical or not, he'd declined her offer to advertise his whereabouts. Later, whenever she'd suggested he ride with her to town and back to see if anything looked familiar, he'd found some excuse not to go. His head was bothering him—or his knee or his ankle, both of which were almost back to normal except for the occasional twinge when he turned too quickly.

The truth was—

Hell, he didn't know what the truth was; he only knew he felt safe here. Until he knew what was out there waiting for him—until he was fully fit, both physically and mentally—he preferred to play it safe.

"Look, why don't I go by to see what the library has on amnesia?" Ellen offered.

"Thanks, but that's not necessary. Now that my headache's almost gone, my memory's showing definite signs of returning."

Neither of which was consistently true, but close enough. His headache was down to a dull, background pressure, and for the past couple of days he'd been…sensing things. Usually it was something on the news or in the daily paper that triggered a reaction.

Now all he had to do was figure out what the reaction meant—waiting, not pushing too hard. No point in confusing himself with a lot of psychobabble.

Then, too, he didn't want Ellen going out of her way to do him any more favors. He already owed her too much. Once his brain came back on line and he was able to pick up his life again, he would be on his way. The first thing he intended to do was to find some way to repay her. Maybe he could find her a couple of good men and pay them under the table. Or maybe he could set up some kind of a fund for Pete. Whatever he did would have to be done tactfully, possibly even secretly. For a lady who was living from day to day, she had more than her share of pride.

Maybe he could arrange to buy a couple of her horses, although where he would keep them, not to mention what use he had for them, remained to be seen.

As did far too much else.

Storm was going over an old newspaper he'd found in the kindling basket a day or so later when Ellen came inside from her morning chores, cheeks glowing and her hair slipping free of the scarf she'd used to tie it back. She was either upset or angry. He recognized that militant march.

"Where's Pete?" he asked, rising from the only man-size chair in the room.

"School. This is Monday, in case you've lost track."

"I thought that was a bus I heard early this morning."

"He hates having to ride it. He's been begging me all year to let him ride his bike to school, but now..."

Right. Now the argument was settled. Probably for the best, as the highway was no place for an eight-year-old on a bike. "Any chance of getting him another one?" He knew the answer before she spoke. She'd admitted to being unable to pay higher wages to attract good help. She was good at disguising it, but the signs of near poverty were everywhere. Beans, macaroni and bologna sandwiches weren't exactly his idea of gourmet fare.

"Maybe for Christmas. I worried about letting him ride it even as far as Joey's, but then, it's not like we're on a major highway."

"Not all the dangers are out on the interstate."

"Oh, I know, you think I'm being overprotective, but—" She gestured helplessly, visible anger seeping away as she crossed the room to hang up her heavy wool shirt. "I hate to deny him anything he really wants when he's already lost so much. And yes, you don't have to say it—I know he has to grow up. It's just that he's all I have. You know how it is." Shrugging, she gestured, palms out, with her calloused hands.

When he didn't reply, she looked at him and bit her lip. "Sorry. I guess you don't."

"No problem." And then, "Yeah, big problem. Look, I can't even offer to pay room and board, much less—"

"Hush! I owe you more than I can ever repay. Pete would've— He told me how he froze, watching that awful thing roaring down at him, with no place to hide even if he'd had time. If anything had happened to him, I don't know what I'd have done."

She turned away, arms hugging her chest as she stared out through the window at the red barn that was in far better shape than the house. He waited, not saying anything because he didn't know what to say. Hell, maybe he had saved the kid's neck, but it hadn't involved any heroics. There hadn't been time for heroics. Truth was, he'd come close to drowning them both in that flooded drainage ditch before Pete had managed to wiggle out from under him.

"How long has it been?" he asked, curious now about more than his own identity.

"How long?" She turned away from the window, arms still wrapped around the bosom she disguised whenever she went out to the barn by wearing a man's shirt. He'd noticed that about her—guessed the reason for it. "If you mean how long have you been here, I've lost track. Let's see, the storm hit last…was it Tuesday or Wednesday?"

"No, I meant how long since your husband…"

"Died? You can say it. I'm not fragile."

She was far more fragile than she cared to admit, but he didn't think she'd like knowing he'd picked up on her vulnerability. A man would have to be blind not to. Blank he might be; blind he was not. "How long have you and Pete lived here alone?"

"Jake died just over two years ago. He was sick for a while before that, and we stayed here as long as we could. The visiting nurse taught me—" Breaking off, she took a deep breath and turned to stare out the window at the high clouds building up out over the Gulf of Mexico.

She'd nursed him at home. It had to have been hellish for her, knowing that the end was inevitable. Somehow, though, he wasn't surprised. "Pete was in the first grade when Jake died," she said, picking up the threads of her story as if determined to lay out all the facts and then move on. "We'd moved here from Laredo. Before that we lived in Dallas. And before that, we were in the army. At least, Jake was. See, we'd been looking for just the right place because Jake's ambition was to breed quarter horses, and we both wanted a place away from town, but close to a good school."

He waited for her to go on, had a feeling she needed to talk. As far as he knew, no one had even come by to see how she'd fared in the tornado, which meant either she hadn't had time to make friends or she'd managed to tick off all her neighbors. She didn't strike him as antisocial, so too busy for much of a social life was his best guess.

Her next words corroborated it. "At first I didn't much like it, with no close neighbors. I mean, I've always had people around. I grew up with lots of friends, and then, in the army, of course, there were the other wives." She bit her lip and he found himself staring at the way her teeth dented the soft, pink flesh. "But once we settled in there wasn't time to think about anything but getting the barn in shape—that was our first priority, then we were going to tackle the house."

He watched her as she talked, seeing the way she used her hands to make a point. She was graceful. Feminine. Even when she was wearing baggy jeans and one of her late husband's shirts.

"Jake always hated the city, but that's where the jobs were. He grew up in a rough section of Dallas and joined the army as soon as he was old enough. He was thinking about making it his career, but then we met and fell in love, and—" Here she paused, twisted the plain gold band on her ring finger, and then shook her head, as if in answer to an unasked question. "I got pregnant and Jake was afraid he'd be sent overseas, so he got out and we went back to Dallas, and Jake went into construction work. He was always good with his hands—he had this way of thinking through a project before he ever started it—sort of a logical mind. Truly, it's a gift. I hope Pete inherited it, but I'm afraid he might have inherited more of my impulsiveness."

"Leap first and look later?" He'd never have pegged her for the impulsive type, not with that square little jaw. On the other hand, she'd hired that pair of scumbags without first checking them out. But that, he suspected, had been more a case of desperation than impulsiveness.

For the first time since he'd erupted into her life—
or she into his—he watched her visibly relax. It was
like seeing a butterfly emerge from a chrysalis and flex
its newfound wings.

And if that was a clue that he was some kind of
poet, then he must be pretty damned good at it to afford
the kind of clothes he'd been wearing.

Clearing his throat, Storm wrenched his mind back
into line and asked, "How far are we from the state
prison?"

Ellen blinked those remarkable green eyes. "The
prison? Several miles, I think. I've never had occasion
to go there. Why?"

He shrugged. "No real reason. Just a feeling I had.
Probably something I heard on the news, I don't
know." He smiled at her then, the kind of smile that
invited a like response. For several long moments he
basked in the spell of her rare answering smile before
turning away, oddly affected without knowing why.
"Just grasping at straws, I guess."

Four

Long after he left the room, his step only slightly uneven as he favored his left leg, Ellen stared after him, thinking. Wondering. Struggling with feelings that veered from gratitude to suspicion to guilt—to something she would prefer not to examine too closely. The kind of tingling awareness she hadn't felt in years. Whoever and whatever he was, anything of that nature was out of the question. She owed him more than she could ever repay, but she really didn't know him.

He'd mentioned the prison. There had been prison gangs out cleaning up after the devastation, she'd heard that on the news—but that was after the tornado, not before. Besides, he would hardly have been a member of a road gang, dressed the way he'd been dressed. Still, he'd had no identification on him, and there hadn't been time to get rid of it. What kind of man traveled without identification?

What kind of woman living alone with her child, with no close neighbors, would bring home a stranger with no identification, one who claimed to have lost his memory? And then, based on instinct alone, turned away two men who might have identified him?

The answer, of course, was a gullible fool. One who had been severely overprotected to the point that she'd grown up feeling like a bird in a gilded cage.

After the only son of a friend had been kidnapped

for ransom, Leonard Summerlin had insisted that Howard, his chauffeur who doubled as a bodyguard, drive Ellen back and forth to school. All her friends had had to be vetted before she could even play with them. Having to bring her boyfriends home to be interrogated by her father had been so embarrassing it was a wonder she'd had had any social life at all.

How she had hated all that. It might even be the reason she had escaped the way she had—by eloping with a man she'd met at the mall when he'd been trying to pick out a birthday gift for a friend's three-year-old daughter. She had slipped her leash to go shopping that April afternoon and literally run headlong into a handsome young soldier who was standing outside a toy store window, trying to decide between a Barbie doll and a toy makeup kit. When he'd seen her staring at him—in a tight-fitting uniform with those shiny brown boots, he'd been well worth a second look—he had asked her what she thought a three-year-old girl would like better, the doll or the makeup kit. That had led to a discussion of baby dolls versus grown-up dolls and she had eventually helped him select a gift more suitable for the child.

After that, she'd done a lot of shopping. Howard would wait at the food court while she sallied forth in the mall. Jake, back in the States on leave, would meet her at the bookstore, which lent itself to leisurely browsing. Once inside, they would study the covers of all the paperbacks and Jake would make up outrageous stories to fit each one. She'd fallen in love with his mind even before she had with his body.

No, that wasn't quite true. She'd fallen in lust about half an hour before she'd fallen in love. Jake had been handsome, shy and protective, not to mention totally unlike any man she had ever met before. What woman could resist such a combination? Certainly not a naive, overprotected college sophomore who had never been exposed at close range to a man who defined the word macho. The uniform had only added to the mystique.

She had trusted her instincts and they hadn't let her down. In spite of the difference in their backgrounds, Jake had wanted to confront her father and ask for her hand. Ellen had nixed that notion immediately. Her father might be a model citizen, a world-class financier and the recipient of more civic awards than his walls would comfortably hold, but he knew too many people in high places. Jake would have suddenly found himself transferred to the South Pole for an extended tour of duty, and before she knew it, she'd have been hustled into a match with her father's ambitious junior partner, Greg Sanders. He of the Gucci loafers and the pungent personalized cologne.

They had eloped, but Jake had insisted on calling her father immediately afterward to tell him she was all right. It was Jake who had notified her father of the change of address each time they'd moved. "In case he should take a notion to come see us," he'd said, and she'd scoffed at the idea. Eight months after she'd married, her father had written to ask if she had come to her senses yet. He had demanded that she move back to Austin. She had ignored that letter as she had done all the rest—four in all—demanding that she return. "I had your tin soldier investigated, and I assure you, you can have no idea what kind of man he really is. What kind of neighborhood he grew up in. He's not our kind of people, Ellen. I blame your lapse in judgment on your mother's side of the family. I'm sure I taught you to be more discriminating."

That was one of her father's favorite forms of discrimination. Anyone who didn't go to the right school, belong to the right clubs, attend the right church or even drive the right kind of car, was "not our kind of people." It used to make her cringe whenever he said it, as often as not in the presence of the staff or some of their children, with whom she used to sneak out to play dolls or jump rope.

Since then she'd had only one occasion to contact her father. When Jake had been so desperately ill and she'd needed money to hire someone to help with Pete. Leonard Summerlin had ignored her pleas, just as she had ignored his letters. Her last contact, three months after Jake had died, had been through his lawyer, who had urged her to reconsider and move back home to Austin.

"Go back and be treated like a recaptured prisoner?" she'd retorted. "No thanks. My father couldn't be bothered to help me the one time I ever asked him for anything. I don't need him now."

"Has he even met your son?" the pin-striped lawyer had asked.

"No, and I don't want him to. He'll insist on taking over every aspect of my son's life the way he did mine after Mama died, and it's not going to happen."

She had learned many things in the years since she had defied her father and been disowned for her efforts—learned to manage money and to do her own housework. Learned to do without things she had once considered necessities. She had learned that she had worth as an individual, completely unrelated to who her father was.

She liked to think of herself as a work in progress. Every day she learned something new. One of the first things she'd learned was to rely on her instincts. So far, they had yet to let her down.

"All right," she told herself now. "Think! Work it out step by step." What if the man she called Storm was actually J. Spencer Harrison, the missing district attorney? Or what if he was only pretending to have lost his memory, but was actually a crook? Not all crooks looked like those two thugs who had turned up on her doorstep the night of the tornado. She knew of one man who had belonged to two of her father's clubs and had actually dined at the Summerlin home, who had later been arrested for laundering money for a drug cartel.

All right, so she didn't have enough information to build a case either way. Instinct or not, she'd do well not to let her impulsive nature lead her into trouble. Pete desperately missed his father, even though he was trying hard not to let on. The last thing he needed was to start thinking of their unexpected guest as a hero and have him turn out to be some awful person who would suddenly disappear from their lives. Or worse.

Of course, he really was a hero, she admitted. Whatever else he was or wasn't, at least he was a gentle man. That much was evident in the way he treated Pete. Most men tended to talk down to children. Storm treated him as an individual, and Pete responded to him the way a puppy responded to a friendly voice.

She just hoped nothing would cause either of them to regret taking him in. Poor Pete had lost too much to risk attachment to a new friend only to lose him, too.

Oddly enough, it never occurred to her to put herself in that same category. Storm was an attractive man— even an intriguing man—but he was only passing through, she reminded herself, not for the first time.

Like one of those gorgeous migratory birds she occasionally saw, wishing it would linger long enough for her to identify.

First thing every morning, as soon as he'd washed the breakfast dishes, Storm took the morning paper and a second cup of coffee into the living room. There were beds to be made and laundry to be done, but he felt a deep compulsion to read every word in the *Mission Creek Clarion*. At this point he was grasping for straws. Too much time had passed and he was still drawing a blank. By now the storm news had been relegated to a few paragraphs in the second section, but sooner or later, something had to ring a bell.

New District Attorney Appointed Following Harrison's Disappearance. The headline was centered on the front page above the fold, accompanied by a photo of a well-dressed, middle-aged man with a skimpy moustache and a bad comb-over. Storm skimmed the pullquote and then returned his attention to the picture, studying every detail. Waiting for something to trigger a reaction. Standard rent-a-bookshelf background. Nothing particularly alarming about the guy, who looked like a typical chamber-of-commerce type. So what was there about the new D. A. that affected him like a hard right to the solar plexus?

Sitting in Ellen's man-size leather chair, in her attractive, if slightly cluttered, slightly shabby living room, he suddenly felt compelled to do something. To collar someone and protest—

Protest what?

He felt the first qualms of nausea. Taking a deep breath, he carefully reread the headline, the pull-quote, then devoured the complete text again. He stared at the photograph of the new district attorney and then he clenched his fists, closed his eyes and began to swear.

J. S. Harrison.

Storm Harrison?

There was a connection there, but until he knew which side of the law he was on, and who he was running from, he'd do well to keep his suspicions to himself.

A few minutes later he rose to begin gathering up the laundry. Ellen's bundle had been carefully sorted and left on the washing machine. She did her own intimate garments, which Storm found amusing. Evidently she'd picked up on the way he was beginning to feel about her. Guilty, for one thing. While the last thing on his mind should be sex with his benefactress, it was growing increasingly hard to see her bursting in through the back door, her silky brown hair windblown and her green eyes sparkling, and not react.

Gratitude would have been an appropriate reaction. Friendship—sure, why not? He knew more about her now than her closest neighbor did—probably even more than her own son. And the more he came to know her, the more he found to like. To admire.

The fact that it wasn't solely friendship he was feeling was inconvenient, to say the least. Even that first night, when his head had felt like a busted melon and she'd come into his room wearing that shabby old bathrobe, shoved up his pajama leg and began massaging liniment into his knee, he'd felt the first stir of sexual awareness. Since then it had grown to the point where he was wary of being alone with her after Pete went to bed. With his mind an empty slate, he found it too easy to fill it with visions of himself following Ellen up those stairs—of Ellen stepping out of the shower and reaching for a towel. Of Ellen tossing restlessly in her bed, which happened to be right above the room he was using.

"Judas priest, man, get a grip!" he muttered as he ran water into the washer, tossed in a pair of his jeans and two pairs of Ellen's, and looked around for Pete's things. He was supposed to have brought them down before leaving for school.

Well, hell, if he could tote a basket full of wet laundry, he could handle a few stairs. All signs of inflammation in both his ankle and his knee had disappeared. The knot on his head was gone. Basically he was good as new, if only he could fill in a few Grand-Canyon-size potholes where his memory was supposed to reside.

He'd quit using the crutch a couple of days ago. Now he held on to the banister, taking one step at a time. No pain, no gain. Where had he heard that before? Did that work in reverse? Because he didn't feel so much as a twinge.

He was grinning triumphantly by the time he reached the top of the stairs. That was, he was grinning until he saw Ellen. She was clutching her bathrobe and a pair of slippers in front of her. Jaybird naked, as far as he could tell.

"Omigod," she blurted.

"I thought you were outside." Stepping back, he grabbed the newel to keep from tumbling down the stairs. He was breathing heavily. From exertion, he told himself, trying hard not to stare at the satiny flesh above the chenille robe.

"What are you doing up here? You're not supposed to tackle stairs yet."

"I could ask you the same thing. I didn't hear you

come inside." To reach her bedroom she would have to pass close by where he was standing.

"I came in the back way. Look, I don't know what you're doing up here, but if it can wait...?" She'd managed to slip her arms into her robe. Now she tightened the sash around her waist.

"Sure. I mean, I was only going to see if Pete had anything to wash. He forgot to bring his things down this morning." Storm couldn't take his eyes off her waist. Couldn't be more than twenty inches—in another era, hers would have been called an hourglass figure.

"Sorry, I didn't mean to stare—only, Ellen, you do know how beautiful you are, don't you?"

Her jaw fell. "I know what? Storm, have you been drinking?"

"Coffee. That's all, I swear. I just thought...I mean—" He shook his head. What did he mean? That she was beautiful? That was a given.

That he would like nothing better than to open her bedroom door, lead her over to her bed and join her there?

Absolutely.

That he was acting like a man who'd lost not only his memory but every grain of decency he'd ever possessed?

Yeah, that, too.

"I slipped and fell down in the manure pile."

The way she was glaring at him, you'd have thought it was somehow his fault. He blinked and tried to control his grin. It was better than rampaging lust, but not a whole lot better. "Soft landing, I hope."

"That damned mare—I think she's going to drop her foal any day now. The vet said they get irritable just before they deliver. Do you call it deliver when it's a horse? Oh, Lord, the things I don't know,'' she said, looking helpless, hopeless, and totally irresistible.

Closing the distance between them, he eased his hands over her shoulders, leaned closer and sniffed. And tried not to laugh. The lady reeked of barnyard effluvia. ''Yeah, I guess you do need a shower. Use all the hot water you need, the laundry can wait.''

She didn't even try to escape, just stared up at him with those changeable green eyes of hers. ''Oh. Um, thanks.''

''And listen, those mares of yours don't care what you call it—they'll come through just fine. We can call the vet and he can either come out or tell us whatever we need to know. We'll set up camp out in the barn if we need to, okay?''

''We?''

''Uh, you. Me, too, if it'll help.''

The way she was staring at him, she must think he'd lost what few wits he'd managed to retain. All she said, though, was, ''I stink. For goodness' sake, let me go wash this smell off. I left my clothes on the back porch, but don't even think about putting them in the wash until I've soaked out the worst of the...the—''

''Essence of horse. You got it. And, Ellen, promise me you'll quit worrying?''

''No, but thanks, anyway. I mean, for caring— I mean, being concerned about—''

''Shh. Caring will do. It'll do just fine.'' And he leaned over the few inches that separated them and kissed her. Gently, holding her away from his body. Better to let her think he was leery of getting too close to the smell of horse manure, than allowing her to realize how she was affecting him. At this rate, it was going to take more than a long cold shower to bring him back down. About a five-mile jog should do it.

The kiss ended almost before it began. He would have liked to explore further—much further—but it was the kind of kiss she needed at the moment. Non-threatening, non-demanding. Just the soft, hesitant press of his mouth to hers.

She stepped back as if just remembering that she was practically naked. "Don't come any closer. I warned you, I stink."

"Yeah, now that you mention it..." Grinning, he turned toward Pete's room. If she thought that was why he hadn't made more of the moment, let her believe it. Better that than she find out that while his head might be screwed up, there was nothing at all wrong with his libido.

Now that he was improving physically, he obviously needed something more demanding than housework to work off excess energy. He would just have to figure out whatever he could manage to do, inexpertly or not, that would wear him out and at the same time allow Ellen to sit and put her feet up for a few minutes. He owed her that much and far more.

What he didn't owe her was to move in on her like a rutting animal. For the first day or so after she'd lugged him home with her, his physical reactions hadn't been so pronounced. She had iced his swollen joints with a sack of frozen peas and rubbed something smelly on the injured flesh. Horse liniment, probably. He must have made a sound the first time, because she had glanced up and asked if it stung.

Looking back, he was pretty sure it hadn't been the liniment that had caused his reaction, nor even the painful pressure of her hands on his swollen flesh. It had been those hands of hers stroking his bare skin while she'd knelt in front of him. Even in the condition he'd been in then, it hadn't taken much memory to know that some things were off limits, no matter how great the temptation.

Ellen was one of those things.

By the end of the week the tornado news had been relegated to a few inches on page thirteen. Dump trucks were still hauling away the ruins of a trailer park and parts of a strip mall. A new steeple was already being built for the church. The warehouse had been reroofed and the dispossessed residents of Shady Grove Trailer Park had been relocated. Storm continued to read the daily newspaper from front page to last, including the classified ads. Still no mention of a missing husband, father, brother, son or business partner. The district attorney was evidently still missing, but after the first few days, there were no more stories.

Strange. He'd have thought it would be big news. Maybe the guy had turned up, in which case he would need to find himself a new identity.

Ellen was in and out during the day while Pete was in school, doing chores that Storm insisted he could be helping her with now that he was physically able again.

"Don't even think about it," she'd insisted right back. "The last thing either of us needs is for you to get kicked by a horse or to slip on a patch of fresh manure the way I did. In your condition, you'd probably be laid up for the rest of the year."

"What do you mean, in my condition? In case you haven't noticed, I'm in peak physical shape now."

She'd stared pointedly at his forehead, noting that the knot was gone, and the bruising had faded to a grayish shade of yellow. "Yeah, yeah, you're ready for the Olympics," she'd jeered softly. "Look, if I have to have more help, I'll call on one of my neighbors."

"Speaking of neighbors, it's been a week now and I haven't noticed any of them coming around to check on you."

"Because they know we're all right. Joey's folks called and I told them—"

"About me?"

She'd hesitated for so long he'd thought she wasn't going to answer. Later he might wonder why. "Look, if you want me to spread the word, letting any interested parties know where to find you, just say so. I offered to do it before, if you'll remember. Maybe I'm wrong, but I got the idea you weren't too eager to advertise your presence until you're back in your right mind."

"Ouch. Did you have to put it that way?"

A smile had tugged at the corners of her mouth. "You know what I mean."

"Yeah, I do. I'm only teasing, Ellen."

She'd sighed then, and flopped onto the sofa. Tugging a plastic jet fighter out from under her left hip, she'd waved the F-18 in a careless gesture, then set it on the coffee table along with two comic books, a copy of *Horse Breeders Quarterly,* a pot holder that had somehow strayed in from the kitchen, and a stoneware vase of dried flowers.

"I guess I'm out of practice. Being teased, I mean. Jake used to tease me about— Oh, you know. Things like not knowing the difference between a holdback horse and a cutting horse. And not liking fried liver and strawberry ice cream."

"Together?"

"Of course not, silly. They're just two foods I don't happen to care for."

"Right. Uh, what is the difference, by the way?"

"The difference?"

"Holdback and cutting."

"Oh. Well, this is book learning, you understand— we never made it to the training part—but from what I've read, a holdback horse is trained to hold back. Actually, they back up. I can give you Jake's books on the subject if you're really interested. Right now, training is the least of my worries. I just want my mares to give me two healthy babies I can either sell or breed when they're old enough. I might eventually hire a trainer, or maybe not. Maybe just producing and selling will be enough."

For several moments neither of them had spoken. It had been an oddly comfortable silence. The kind that occurs when two people know each other well. Although just how he could be so certain of that, he couldn't have said. All the same, he knew he liked her company. Liked looking at her. Liked talking to her. Would have liked doing more than looking under other circumstances.

She'd turned to him then, picked up the plane again, and he could have sworn she'd been about to say something important. Instead, she'd shaken her head, murmured something about locating a spool of wire and gone back outside.

Five

What, Storm wondered idly, had Ellen been about to tell him? That it was time he left? That she didn't like the way he made the beds? That he'd used too much detergent in the laundry? He'd figured that much out by himself when the suds had threatened to overflow. Figured it out and dealt with it. He still had a few gray cells on active duty.

Feeling restless—his usual state these days—Storm opened the front door and studied the terrain. Nothing unusual about it. Nothing in the least outstanding, yet he liked it.

As compared to what? a mocking voice asked.

Okay, so the partial fence around the house needed painting. For that matter, the house itself needed painting. Maybe while he was here he could—

And maybe not.

The remnants of a sadly neglected lawn cried out for help. Someone—Ellen, probably—had planted some ornamental shrubs that were also in need of attention. Maybe if he picked up a pair of pruning shears, something would come back to him.

The horse barn was in surprisingly good shape compared to the other outbuildings. Among other things, she needed a carpenter. He had a feeling that memory or not, he was not now, nor had he ever been, a carpenter.

However, he might as well try his hand at a few simple repairs. It didn't take a college degree to tighten a few hinges so that gates wouldn't sag and shutters wouldn't bang against the wall. Given the right tools, common sense should kick in and tell him how to make a few basic repairs.

His gaze shifted to the lane, which was badly in need of resurfacing. He had a vague memory of being bumped over a few potholes, tilting dangerously and grabbing hold of the metal sides of the wheelbarrow when Ellen and Pete had steered him around others.

At the other end of that driveway there was a state highway. A hedgerow blocked the view, but he could hear the sound of traffic quite clearly from where he stood. Somewhere out there he had a vehicle, or what was left of one. He had to have been driving. His memory was hazy, but he didn't recall seeing a car nearby when he'd been dragged out of that ditch.

Ellen had mentioned seeing a delivery van a few hundred yards down the highway. Later she'd seen a wrecked pickup and the hood of a red sports car.

Could any of them have been his?

Possibly. Whatever he'd been driving, there was bound to be some form of ID in it. License plates could be traced. Had anyone done that? And if not, damn it, why not?

Had he been alone when the twister struck?

Unable to find answers, his restless mind returned to his immediate surroundings. From where he stood he could see one corner of the paddock where two mares swished away the flies. Nice-looking stock. Nothing outstanding, but good, serviceable mounts. It occurred to him that he'd never seen Ellen or Pete up on one.

Still, they had to be saddle broken. Maybe he could buy one of the geldings and ride out of here.

Oh, yeah? Using what for money? For all he knew, he couldn't even ride. It was really beginning to gall the hell out of him, being out of the loop.

Stealing a horse to escape was probably not an option. Whatever else he was—or wasn't—he was pretty sure he was no horse thief.

Wearing shoes that had dried stiff, the soles curling up slightly at the toes, he made his way carefully down the front steps and crossed the clearing between house and barn. From inside he could hear Ellen raising hell with one of the hands. If it was the one he'd already met, the jerk probably deserved it.

"I don't care who did it, it wasn't done properly, so you'll just have to do it over."

"It was done good enough. If it didn't hold, it's 'cause yer posts is too rotted to hold a fencing nail. That ain't my fault. You didn't say nothin' 'bout replacin' no posts."

Storm felt his hands curling into fists. Should he step in and back her up? He was almost up to fighting trim. He outweighed the bastard by a good fifty pounds. On the other hand, Ellen could probably take him if he didn't interfere. Any woman who could manage to haul a full-grown man up out of that ditch and get him to her house with only the aid of a wheelbarrow and a skinny kid could easily handle a whining runt like—

"Where's Clyde?" she demanded.

Okay, so this must be the other one. Buster? Booker. And she was steaming, all right. Without raising her voice, she managed to get her point across.

"Gone to the feed store. Reck'n he'll stop by the diner after that."

"The bar, you mean. He can drink on his own time. I want that fence back up by dark today. If it's not—"

Storm figured if there was ever a time to interfere, this was it. He might not know his own name, but even he could recognize the hollowness behind her threat. She could fire the pair of them and then do all the work herself. That insolent jackass knew it, too. He was sprawled across a bale of hay, smirking openly.

About to stride through the barn door—at least he could stride now without hobbling—he was ready to jerk a knot in Booker's scrawny neck when he heard the sound of a car turning into the lane.

He could also hear Ellen, still loaded for bear, moving to the door to see who was headed up the driveway. Catching sight of Storm in the doorway, she shook her head in a signal he had no trouble reading. *Butt out. I can handle this.*

Ellen Wagner might be a lot of things, he thought, somewhat amused, mostly concerned. Superwoman, she wasn't. The insolent bastard with the greasy ponytail hadn't made the first move to round up any fencing tools. Just as she turned to go meet whoever was headed up her lane, he'd spat a stream of tobacco juice that landed not six inches from where she'd been standing.

The slimeball grinned openly. When Ellen marched past Storm, he heard her mutter something like, "Damn it, what now?"

Striding into the barn, he reached down, grabbed a fistful of dirty shirt and lifted the jerk up onto his toes.

Booker's grin wavered and disappeared. "Hey, put me down! You can't do that!"

"Listen closely, you creep, I'll say this once. The

next time you feel the urge to spit, you swallow instead, you got that?'' Storm leaned in close, then backed off as the stench of bad teeth and an unwashed body struck him. Still holding on to a fistful of filthy, faded flannel, he said, "Did that register? Good. Now pay careful attention. You will mend that fence. Those staples will hold, do I make myself clear?''

"Man, it ain't my fault her posts is rotten," Booker whined.

Storm released him suddenly and dusted off his hands. Looking aggrieved, the hired man staggered, sputtering his outrage. Storm shut him up with a single look, a talent he hadn't known he possessed.

Had Ellen known her fence needed replacing and not just repairing? If so, she should have had supplies on hand. The fact that she hadn't was one more indication that the lady was hanging on by a shoestring.

The trouble was, there wasn't much he could do to help her, short of recovering his memory, learning that he could afford it and ordering a truckload of fencing material and sufficient labor to utilize it. Two dozen roses and a bottle of good wine might make a nice hostess gift, but in this case, a truckload of fence posts would probably be more appreciated.

Booker started to sit again, thought better of it and slouched against the wall, working on a ragged thumbnail.

"Do we have an understanding?" Storm pressed.

"Yeah, yeah. Soon's Clyde gets back, me'n him'll go fix the sonovabitchin' fence, but I can tell you right now, mister, it ain't gonna hold."

"It'll hold." As long as he was bluffing, he might as well do a thorough job of it. "I'll be riding out first thing in the morning to check on it. The job had better

be done by then. Use baling wire instead of staples if
you have to, but make it hold.''

Not until he was halfway across the yard to where
Ellen was standing did it occur to him that he knew
how to jury-rig an old fence line. Hooray. One piece
of the puzzle had fallen into place. Now all he had to
do was find roughly a million more and fit them together.

As if in need of support, Ellen waited beside Pete's
basketball standard for the visitor to negotiate her rutted drive. Her arms were crossed in a familiar posture.
If he read her right—and he was getting pretty good at
it—she was definitely playing defense.

Shoving his anger to a back burner, he moved up
beside her in case this turned out to be another creep
who got his jollies from jerking women around. His
heart was pumping adrenaline by the gallon.

She moved a step closer, her arms still crossed de-
fensively over her breasts, but otherwise ignored him.

''You expecting company?'' he asked quietly.

''Not this kind of company.'' While he was still pon-
dering that, she added, ''Are you?''

''Well now, I could've sworn the party invitations
said half past four. Looks like I'll have to hire a new
social secretary.''

After a brief, astonished look, she laughed, which
had been the whole point of the lame joke. She'd been
looking as if one more straw would have broken the
camel's back, and while he might not be able to slay
all her dragons, the least he could do was provide a
touch of comic relief.

Turning his attention to the visitor, it occurred to
him that this could be someone looking for him.
The leap of anticipation was only slightly tainted

by...disappointment? Hell, that didn't even make sense.

Instead of stopping beside the shed where the trucks were parked, the car pulled up in front of the picket fence, its gleaming presence distinctly out of place against the backdrop of shaggy shrubs and peeling white paint. Together they waited for the doors to open. "You think maybe this is another member of the silk-underwear-and-monogrammed-handkerchief set?" he inquired softly, still playing for laughs.

Tongue in cheek, she looked him over, from the tips of his ruined cordovans to the top of his shaggy head, taking in the faded jeans he wore low on his hips to make up for the lack of length and her husband's flannel shirt that didn't quite accommodate his shoulders. "If it is, I'm not sure he'll recognize you. Have any of your friends ever seen you before with a yellow and lavender forehead?"

Standing close enough to feel the heat of her body, close enough to catch a whiff of alfalfa hay and the baby powder he knew she dusted down with after her shower, Storm waited for the visitor to emerge. It was probably just someone pulling in off the highway to check his map or to ask directions. It didn't take a genius to recognize the make and model as one usually indicative of a seven-figure income. Whether that had any meaning or not, he couldn't have said. The information just popped into his head.

And then the door began to open and Ellen muttered, "Oh, hell."

"Is that good or bad?"

Her fingers dug into his arm and he covered her hand with his own as a good-looking, fortyish blond guy wearing madras slacks, a linen blazer and a pair of aviator-style sunglasses emerged, one long leg at a time.

Ellen pulled her arm free and moved toward the car. "Greg," she said calmly, just as if she hadn't been spitting nails only moments before.

"Ellen, it's been a while."

Smooth, Storm thought, sizing him up and filing away the details as if he'd done it a thousand times. With nothing more than instinct to base an opinion on, he didn't trust the man. If Ellen expected him to walk off and leave her alone with her guest, she'd have to speak up.

Her guest, not someone looking for him. Storm didn't know whether he was relieved or disappointed. Some of both, probably. He was definitely curious. She introduced the guy as Greg Sanders, a business associate of her father's.

"Greg, this is Storm—Hale," she said.

He nearly lost it. Storm Hail? It occurred to him then that they hadn't bothered to give him a last name. She'd been forced to improvise or to tell the truth. Evidently she'd picked up on his reluctance to explain the situation, but that didn't mean she had to go along with it. It was her call to make.

She didn't make it. At least, not yet.

A business associate of her father's, hmm? What kind of business was her father in, anyway? Not ranching—not unless he was a lot more successful than his daughter. And if she had a father in the business—in any business—what the devil was he doing allowing his daughter to struggle along with only the help of a couple of slugs like Clyde and Booker?

When an awkward pause occurred during which Storm knew damned well Sanders expected him to take a hike, he offered to go make coffee. Not lunch, although it was past time and neither of them had eaten. There was a limit to his generosity.

To Ellen's generosity, he amended when she murmured that that would be lovely.

Lovely? Were we playing lady now?

He hesitated, trying to read the scene and to get a handle on the players. Sanders's smile would have done credit to a barracuda. "I just happened to be in neighborhood and thought I'd come by and see how you were getting on. Your father asked me to drop off a few things." He gestured to the trunk of his car.

Ellen shook her head. "You can tell my father thanks, but no thanks."

"He'll be disappointed."

"Will he?"

Storm waited for a response. The brief exchange seemed to imply far more than the words actually said.

They strolled toward the house, with Storm acting as rear guard. Ellen led her guest into the living room, making no effort to collect Pete's scattered toys, a coffee cup and the morning papers, which were folded over the arm of a chair. Storm lingered in the hall, not a part of the company, yet unwilling to leave her alone until he knew she could handle things.

Sanders moved to the fireplace and turned to face the room, deliberately assuming the power position. Some men were easy to read, even without a frame of reference. The photograph of Jake Wagner with the stallion, Zeus, was just to the left of the brass and mahogany clock, a few inches from Sanders's linen-clad elbow. Storm had studied the photo enough to form an opinion that Ellen's late husband had been a pretty decent guy. He'd probably have liked him if they'd ever met.

Sanders didn't give it so much as a glance. "How's the boy? He's what—about nine now?"

"He's fine." Pete was eight. She didn't bother to correct him.

Sanders nodded, then sauntered across the room to claim the chair Storm usually sat in. Jake's chair.

"Glad to hear it. Your father sent him a football and some video games."

"Pete likes baseball. He doesn't have time for video games."

"Doesn't have time?" One of Sanders's blond, well-groomed eyebrows lifted in disbelief. "Surely he's not in school that long. Don't you have Christmas holidays coming up soon?"

Storm stood in the hall and looked from one to the other, watching the duel to see who drew first blood. His money was on Ellen.

"He has chores. And homework, even during the holidays. And anyway, he'd rather be outdoors riding or shooting baskets than holed up in the house with a…a gadget."

"Oh, Ellen, sweetheart, you've been out here in the boonies too long. Some of these little gadgets, as you call them, cost more than—"

"I don't care how much they cost, Greg. You can go back and report to my father that we're fine, just fine. We don't need his money, we don't need his gifts, we don't need anything."

Way to go, lady, Storm applauded silently.

"Did you know your father had remarried recently?"

"I don't keep up with his social life."

"No, I don't suppose you do."

As Storm watched the sportily dressed man, noting his swift surveillance of the comfortable if slightly shabby room, another piece of the puzzle came into focus. There was no mistaking the disdain he saw on features that might have been called patrician in another era. Personally, he preferred to call them arrogant, even somewhat effeminate.

So he was good at reading expressions. It was a skill that might serve him well if he happened to be a dealer in a gambling casino or a professional fortune-teller.

Which, for all he knew, he might be.

Turning away, he left to go make coffee before he said something he might regret. Or rather, that Ellen might regret. He was on shaky enough ground here without making things worse.

He lingered in the kitchen until the coffeemaker signaled its readiness, then carried the tray into the living room. Conversation ceased abruptly when he entered. He probably should have found some excuse to leave again, but for some reason he felt like staying close. *Hey, don't mind me, folks, I'm harmless.*

He didn't feel harmless. No way.

Sanders asked about her stock, and she told him about the horses. "I know it's not an ideal mix—we wanted four mares and a stallion, but while we were looking this lot went on sale at a price that was too good to pass up. Jake said we'd need the geldings for riding anyway. So we're starting with just two mares for now. We'll pick up more stock as soon as I can—"

Afford it, Storm filled in mentally.

"—add onto the horse barn," Ellen finished.

Sure we will. No problem.

Storm knew most of the story by now and could guess at the rest. Just about the time Wagner had bought the first of his stock and got them settled in, repaired the barn, built new stalls, patched up the fences and improved the pastures, the bottom had fallen out of their world. After that, every penny had been designated for Wagner's medical treatment. Veterans' benefits would stretch only so far.

Sanders plucked the creases in his madras slacks and crossed his long legs. He wore loafers. "Do you remember the year we all went to the derby?" he drawled. "You were what, about sixteen then?"

Sixteen. Storm tried to picture her at that age. She probably hadn't been a knockout. Gawky, young for her age, probably shy. Some girls matured later than others. Odds were, she'd been a late bloomer.

"No, I don't remember."

And then his eyes narrowed. Either he was getting some mixed signals or he'd lost more than his memory. Ellen didn't want to talk over old times with this guy. Didn't want to talk about anything, if he was reading her correctly. She was getting antsy, and that wasn't like the calm, capable woman he had come to know and admire.

So he jumped into the conversation. "Did you hear about the twister that came through here last week? Any tear through your neighborhood?" It was a leading question. He wasn't sure where he wanted it to lead. Out the front door, preferably.

"I heard about it. The networks all covered it pretty thoroughly. I happened to be watching— Actually, I was out in San Diego at the time. The tennis match, you know? Looks like you got lucky here, El."

Ellen caught his eye, and Storm was amazed to see

a slight smile tug at the corners of her mouth. "Indeed," was all she said.

Storm leaned back in the Boston rocker and sipped his coffee. Like cooking, he hadn't stopped the first time to wonder whether or not he knew how to brew the stuff, he'd just done it. Damned good coffee, too, if he did say so.

"Why don't I unload the things your father sent and you can go through them at your leisure?" Sanders asked.

"No."

"That's it? You won't reconsider? Ellen, the man is your father. He's not getting any younger. Don't you think—"

"My father knows how I feel about his...his generosity. Maybe his new bride can play with the video games when she's not shopping."

"Ouch," Sanders said softly.

Zinger, Storm thought admiringly.

"You always did have a way with words. Well, I suppose I'd better be leaving. Dinner date—the mayor, a state senator, the usual suspects. You know how boring these things can be."

She did?

The newcomer sent him a somewhat puzzled glance, which Storm returned with equanimity. "Haven't we met before, Hale? The name doesn't ring any bells, but I could swear I've seen you somewhere. Do you play golf?"

Storm sat up and carefully placed his cup on a side table. "Not much time for golf lately, I'm afraid," he said, implying that he might or might not have played in the past. Hell, how did he know whether or not he played golf? Put a club in his hand and maybe something would register.

Sanders nodded. "I'm playing in that fund-raiser at the Lone Star Country Club. I do a lot of that sort of thing. Good business, you know. For some reason, you looked familiar, but then, you meet so many people."

"Yeah, you do, don't you?"

"What did you say you did, Hale?"

"Actually, I don't believe I said, but I'm a writer. Fiction."

"Anything I might have read?"

"I doubt it. I write romances."

Ellen choked on her coffee, and by the time she could speak again, Sanders was at the door. Having whacked her on the back a couple of times, Storm let his arm rest on her shoulder as they saw the visitor off. As she didn't protest, he figured she needed all the support she could get.

What he needed was answers. One way or another, he was going to have them.

They watched the heavy black sedan drive off, scraping the tailpipe on some of the deeper ruts, then wordlessly, they turned back inside. Ellen collected the cups and spoons and placed them on the tray. Storm took the tray and headed for the kitchen. She followed him, frowning slightly.

"That was…interesting," he observed, returning the cream to the refrigerator.

"Oh, go ahead and say it. He's a shallow, pretentious jerk. He's always been a shallow, pretentious jerk, probably always will be. And you're wondering who he is and what he was doing here, and how on earth I ever came to know someone like him."

That wasn't exactly what he was wondering, but it

would do for a start. "He's your father's business associate, right? And you've known him ever since you were sixteen? That's reason enough for him to look you up while he's in the neighborhood." He'd be willing to bet it wasn't the whole story, though. The undercurrents would have defeated an Olympic-class swimmer.

She forced a smile. "I haven't seen Greg in— Goodness, it's been almost twelve years."

Storm remained silent. A question now would be counterproductive, and for some reason he wanted to know more about the man, more about their relationship—their former relationship—and why the guy had turned up just now. On the surface it had been a simple friendly visit. He'd been in the neighborhood, hadn't seen her in a long time. Perfectly natural for him to drop by. And incidentally, drop off a few gifts from her father.

But if he was a business associate of her father's, why hadn't they seen each other in years? Why was it she couldn't afford to replace rotten fence posts or hire someone to do a few simple repairs around the house, while her father's associate dined with politicians and drove a late-model luxury sedan.

Why did she refuse to even look at whatever it was her father had sent? Something more than a few toys, he suspected.

She reached for the coffeepot, poured herself another half cup and spooned in more sugar. "You're probably wondering about a few things."

"You could say I'm mildly curious."

"I could tell you it was none of your business, too, but—"

"But rudeness isn't your style."

Looking up, she smiled, but the smile didn't quite make it as far as her eyes. "In case you hadn't noticed, I don't have a style. I'm sorry if Greg made you uncomfortable. Maybe you should have told him about your amnesia and questioned him, since he seemed to recognize you."

"Funny thing—and don't ask me how I know this—but there are some people I'd as soon not be recognized by, if you'll forgive the terminal preposition."

Ellen had known for days that she'd have to tell him. She'd been waiting for an opening, for a good time. There was no good time, and this was as close to an opening as she was likely to have. "Storm, there's something you need to know."

And so she told him. After describing both men and repeating verbatim everything that had been said— she'd gone over it so many times in her mind that remembering was no problem—she waited for him to explode.

"Harrison," he said after a long silence. "J. S. Harrison, as in Jason Spencer Harrison."

Leaning forward, Ellen nearly knocked over her coffee cup. "You remember? Oh, Storm."

His expression was one of resignation more than defeat. "Sorry. I've gone all through the phone book. There are at least a dozen Harrisons, some with J, some with S—even one with both. Turned out to be a lady named Janet Shaw Harrison. Retired schoolteacher. I lied and said I'd like her honest opinion about the local schools, and she gave me an earful."

"Oh, Lord." Ellen lowered her face to her hands and snickered.

"Look, I could call and ask each one if they're missing a relative, but until I can put all the pieces together, I don't think that's particularly wise.''

"But if you're the missing district attorney—''

"Ellen, listen to me. Not to put too fine a point on it, but from the way you described that pair that showed up here looking for me—for someone, at any rate— odds are they weren't exactly selling Girl Scout cookies. All along, I've had a strong feeling of…I don't know, of something.'' He broke off and swore softly in exasperation. "The state prison. Something to do with the state pen. Until I find out which side of the bars I belong on, I don't think it's smart to advertise my presence, so if you're asking for absolution, you've got it. You might even have saved my neck.''

"Oh, for heaven's sake, you're not a crook. I've lived with you long enough to know you're a good man, a decent man. Personally, I think you're that missing D. A. It's just too big a coincidence—the initials and everything. As for the other J. S. Harrison, you'd probably have an unlisted number if you really were the district attorney. But whatever else is going on in your life right now, you're certainly no friend of that pair who came looking for you.''

"In that case, why were they looking for me?''

She shook her head.

"Okay, I'll give you three choices. One, you're wrong about my identity and they're really friends of mine. Or two, they're on the run, and they were looking to steal a car.''

"Oh, hush up, that doesn't even make sense! They already had a car.''

"Too easy to identify. Look, if you're right and they're the bad guys and I'm the good guy, why would they come looking for me? Seems to me, even with my impaired sensibilities, they'd be running hard in the opposite direction. The border's just a hop, skip and a jump from here.''

They were both silent as his words sank in. Ellen said, ''What's the third choice?''

''More of an option than a choice. Until I get this mess figured out, I'd like to stay here, if it's all the same to you. Whoever I am, whatever I'm mixed up in, I have a strong feeling that making a sudden public appearance might set off a chain reaction I'm not ready to deal with.''

Great choice, he thought bitterly, sponging off a woman who was too short of money and too long on pride.

''Of course you're going to stay here. I can't let you leave until—well, until you know where you're going.''

Not to mention a few other bits of vital information. ''Thank you. Then if you don't mind, we'll go on the same way we have been, with you and Pete and that worthless pair of barn rats doing all the heavy lifting while good old Storm makes a mess of trying to keep house and do the cooking.''

''Oh, but you don't have to—''

''Do we have a deal?''

''I suppose so.'' And then, green eyes snapping, she added, ''Of course we have a deal!''

''Good. Now, back to your old friend Greg. I had the distinct impression you weren't too happy to see him. Anything you'd like to share?''

''Not really. At least nothing I can't handle.''

He waited, then drawled softly, ''Right. Like you handled Booker.''

She twiddled with the coffee spoon, not meeting his

eyes, which wasn't like her, so he waited a couple more beats. He'd discovered that it was an effective tactic.

"What makes you think I wasn't glad to see him?"

"You weren't exactly rolling out the Welcome mat. The man came bearing gifts, yet I'm the one who had to invite him inside for refreshments."

"I was…surprised, that's all."

"That's not all, Ellen, but you're right—it's none of my business. Point conceded."

She managed to smile, looking closer to tears than amusement. Or maybe he was reading too much into nothing. That was the trouble with straining to read a blank slate, you were apt to read all sorts of mysterious implications in a scratch or a flyspeck.

"Look, my father and I are…estranged. And if you must know, Greg's the man I was supposed to marry."

His spoon clattered into the saucer. "What? You were engaged to that…that stuffed shirt?"

This time her smile was genuine. "Actually, we never quite got that far. I was supposed to graduate first, at which time my family would announce the engagement with proper fanfare. Then, after a suitable period, we were to marry. A small exclusive wedding, no more than three or four hundred carefully selected guests, followed by a couple of weeks in Bermuda or maybe Paris. After that, Greg would be made a full partner and I would take my place among Austin's young married set, with all that entailed."

An edge of bitterness colored her voice. He'd heard weariness before—weariness, suspicion, tenderness and amusement. The bitterness was new. He didn't like it.

"But then I ruined everything by not following the

rules,'' she said with a whimsical little half smile that tore something inside him.

''I take it you met someone else. Jake?''

Ellen turned her cup in her hands. Callused hands, the short nails clean but unpolished. He waited. Sometimes you had to prime the pump, sometimes you didn't. It all depended on how much pressure had built up.

''You have to understand how it was. Daddy wasn't always so paranoid, but after the son of one of his closest friends was kidnapped and held for ransom, my freedom was cut off like you wouldn't believe. No more tooling around town in my own car, I had to be driven everywhere. To the mall, to the club—even to the dentist.''

Her soft bleat of laughter held little amusement. ''Know what? I discovered a talent I didn't even know I possessed. I got to be an expert on slipping my leash. It never once occurred to Daddy that I might not obey his rules, which only proves he didn't know me at all.''

She fell silent, and it was all Storm could do not to lead with a question. A few moments later she continued. ''But then, I didn't know him very well, either. After my mother died, he waited less than six months to start dating again. If you can call it dating. It was more like he'd take these trips, you know? I was never invited, not that I'd have gone—I mean, what girl needs to watch her father make out? Still, it would've been nice to be asked. They usually started with Paris. All Daddy's girlfriends liked to shop there.''

Storm let the words flow over him and found to his surprise that he was able to visualize a lot of what she described. Not that he thought he'd had an overprotective father. Hell, he didn't know if he'd had one at all, other than biologically.

He learned more about Jake—about the man in the snapshot she had framed and placed on her mantel. And yeah, he thought again that he would have liked him, although they probably wouldn't have had much in common.

Except for Ellen. Except for a taste for women whose subtle, understated beauty would long outlast the high-maintenance kind that probably appealed to jerks like Greg Sanders.

"Looking back, I'm pretty sure the only reason Greg agreed to get engaged to me was because he wanted that partnership. I guess I sensed it even then. He and Daddy had pretty much the same kind of taste when it came to women. Young, blond, gorgeous and sophisticated, all of which I was not. Except for young, I suppose. Too young in some ways."

"Did you resent it? Your father's other women, I mean?"

After a few seconds she said, "You know, I'm not sure. We were never close, but I suppose I'd have resented any woman taking my mother's place, even though I can hardly even remember her. If you mean did I resent Greg's women, I honestly don't know. I knew he was seeing others even when we were about to become engaged. I guess if it had really bothered me I'd have tried to do something about it."

"Such as?"

"Well, what woman doesn't want to be beautiful?" Her smile was droll, self-deprecating. "The trouble is, bleached hair takes too much maintenance and I'm afraid of the knife, so plastic surgery was out. I'm stuck with plain brown hair, a nose that's too short and a mouth that's too big. Not to mention the lack of a few strategic implants.''

''Oh, lady, you underestimate yourself,'' he said softly, and she wrinkled her nose at him.

Tilting back her chair, she exhaled as if sharing the load had relieved some of the pressure that had built up inside her. It occurred to him that every woman needed one close friend to talk to, to share with, to confide in. He had to wonder if there was anyone like that for Ellen.

''I take it you and your father haven't yet buried the hatchet?''

''The last time I saw my father was nearly ten years ago. I read about him occasionally, but we don't really communicate.'' She fell silent.

He watched her for a while, and then said, ''Ellen?''

''It's almost time for the schoolbus. I'd better—''

She started to rise, but Storm blocked her way. Gripping her shoulders, he said, ''Ellen, I'm sorry. For what it's worth, I'm really sorry.''

Her eyes were suddenly too bright. ''Why? It's hardly your fault.''

''No, it's not, but I'm sorry all the same. Can't friends empathize?''

''Friends,'' she said, and then the dam broke. The tip of her nose turned red, her eyes overflowed, and by the time the first sob escaped, his arms were around her and he was holding her, rocking her gently from side to side, murmuring wordless sounds meant to comfort, to soothe.

He had a feeling it wouldn't last long, her need for comfort. All too soon she'd be back to worrying about things like fence posts and bank balances, and roofs with shingles that were beginning to curl. And gifts from her wealthy father that pride alone would not permit her to accept.

His chin brushed against her silky hair. His body responded with embarrassing enthusiasm. He wondered if she'd thought as much about sex as he had over the past few days...and nights. Had she taken a lover since she'd become a widow?

He told himself that holding her was enough, feeling the warmth and strength of her body, her arms clinging to his waist. But this time it wasn't going to work. His lips brushed her cheek and the tip of her ear, and she turned her face ever so slightly so that her eyelashes brushed against his lips. Every cell in his body went immediately to standby alert.

Did she feel it, too? Was she ready for more than simple comfort? More than friendship? Could she possibly be seeking what he was so eager to offer?

The sound of footsteps pounded up the front steps. The door clattered against the wall as Pete came bursting inside. "Hey, guess what?" he yelled, shedding his coat on the floor, slinging his books in the general direction of the hall table. "I passed my—"

And then he was standing in the kitchen doorway. "Mom? What's wrong?"

Six

They were working together in the barn, finishing up the stalls and leading the horses inside. Pete continued to cast Storm questioning looks from time to time, but at least the boy was no longer scowling.

"Did you know that guy? That friend of my mom's?"

They had told him only that an old friend of his mother's from her hometown had stopped by for a brief visit, and that his mother had been feeling homesick.

"Like when I used to have to change schools in the middle of the year and I always hated it?" he'd asked.

"Something like that," Ellen had conceded, and Storm had nodded in silent agreement. He wasn't nearly as embarrassed as he probably should have been.

"I'd never met him before," Storm said now as he pitched in a forkful of clean hay and let the boy spread it. The work should have been done by the two hired hands, but they were still out working on the fence—as far as anyone knew.

"I pro'ly wouldn't have liked him."

"Probably not."

"Yeah. Okay, but don't you dare make my mom cry or anything like that. I take care of my mom."

"I never doubted it for a moment," the tall, solemn man said gravely.

As the last of his doubts dissipated, Pete shot him a

grin full of eight-year-old charm. "Boy, that was one
hell of a storm you and me got caught in, wasn't it?
This kid at my school says a tractor trailer full of grapefruit turned over real near his house and all these cars
skidded in the gunk and man, was it a hell of a mess!"

Ignoring the profanity, Storm spoke thoughtfully.
"I'm not sure if a tornado is classed as a storm. Now,
you take a hurricane—"

"You ever been in one of them? A hurricane?"

"Ah..."

"Oh, yeah. You don't remember. Joey's been in lots
of hurricanes. He used to live in Galveston. Joey says
you have to take pre—pre—"

"Precautions?" Storm filled in. As Ellen brought in
the two geldings, he stepped forth and took one of the
lead lines, moving the horse into the stall they had just
finished cleaning. It never occurred to him that he
might not be able to handle horses, he simply did it.

"Yeah, that's it," Pete picked up where he'd left off
and went on to regale the two grown-ups with the wisdom of his hurricane-wise friend. "Joey's got three
cats, only two of them are babies. Mom, did you know
cats can swim?"

"No, I didn't know that." Using a pick, she was
cleaning out one of the mare's hooves.

"I'd rather have a dog, but I wouldn't mind having
a pet cat?" It was a question. Storm waited to see how
she'd answer it. There were cats slinking around the
barn, but none seemed particularly friendly.

Why not a house cat? he wondered. Or better yet, a
pup? He'd have to remember to inquire sometime when
Pete wasn't around. It might be an issue between them,
one that could do without outside meddling.

The geldings were calm. The mare called Miss Sara

was feeling frisky, but Storm found he could handle her easily. Unselfconsciously, he began to talk to her, stroking her long, sleek neck. When she responded by nudging his shoulder, he promised her a treat.

"She likes apples," Pete said. "Mom said she likes carrots, too. I tried her with broccoli. Yuck! She hates it."

Storm cuffed the boy's head gently. "Better not let your mom see you palming off your vegetables on the horses. She'll double your rations."

"Double yuck," the boy said, grinning to show a pair of oversize front teeth.

"Is Zeus's stall ready?" Ellen called through the door. "I'm going to raise the dickens with that lazy pair of no-goods when they get back from mending that fence. They know what's supposed to get done first, and they didn't muck out a single stall this morning." She brought in the stallion, whose disposition matched his name.

Pete measured out oats. He said, "I know what precautions means. It means putting everything up where the tide can't reach it, and the wind can't blow it away. Joey says—"

With half an ear, Storm listened to the secondhand wisdom while he waited for Ellen to maneuver the big stallion into his stall. She wasn't entirely comfortable with him, but she remained firm. Treated him, in fact, much the way she did her son. She had already brushed him down outside. "I haven't cleaned his hooves yet, but Clyde can do it when he gets in. Believe it or not, he's pretty good with horses."

"Racetracks."

"Pardon?" She dropped the bar across the bottom

half of the double door and glanced around the barn to see what else needed doing.

"Nothing—he just struck me as the type to hang around the track, doing odd jobs. There's a name for them, but for the life of me, I can't remember what it is."

"But you know about it—about racetracks. That's something, at least."

Stroking the nose of one of the mares, he looked thoughtful for a moment. "What about it? Think I'm too big to be a jockey?"

"About twelve inches too tall and fifty or sixty pounds too heavy. How about a trainer? There's no weight limit there."

He considered it. Actually thought about it, then slowly shook his head. "I don't think so. I'm pretty comfortable around these hay processors, but it doesn't feel quite right."

On the other hand, there was a lot of loose money floating around racetracks. And lots of guys who answered the description of that pair who'd come looking for him. One more reason to lay low until he knew which way the wind blew.

"An owner, then. Actually, you were dressed more like an owner when I found you. Except for the mud, of course."

He liked the way she could joke about it. Any day now, he figured, things would start to come back. Maybe it would all pop into focus at once, and then he'd be on his way to...wherever.

But he'd be back. He would make a point of returning because if ever he'd met a lady who needed a friend, it was Ellen Wagner. He could be that friend. He would like to be that friend. Who knows, he mused, leaning against the handle of the pitchfork in the warm, uncomplicated ambience of the big old horse barn, maybe they could even be more than friends.

Right. And maybe he had a wife and kids waiting for him to come back from wherever—a business trip, more than likely.

"Mom, I've finished my chores, so can I go over to Joey's? We're gonna bat some balls. Did you know Mr. Ludlum used to play first base in Triple A?"

"Have you done your homework?"

"Aw, Mom..."

"Spelling and math. Do those and then we'll see."

"Will you take me in the truck?"

"If you get busy on your homework right now, I'll drive you over. You'll have an hour before dark."

After Pete raced out, Storm lifted the wheelbarrow and started out to dump the last load on the manure pile. "Does he usually walk? I thought it was a couple of miles."

"It is. He usually rides his bike, but of course..."

"Right. When's his birthday?"

"September."

"I guess it'll have to be Christmas, then. Unless you had bike insurance?"

By the time Ellen returned from dropping Pete off at his friend's house, Storm had supper under way. Somewhat to his surprise, he seemed to know his way around a kitchen pretty well. He knew the basics, at least: thawing and microwaving.

She dropped into a red-enameled chair that had been painted to match the trim on the white cabinets. If the kitchen had ever been redecorated, it hadn't been recently. More of Pete's art was pinned to the checkered curtains. "You didn't have to do that," she said, but he could tell she was tired. The unexpected visit from an old acquaintance and the run-in by proxy with her father had evidently been the last straw in a day filled with last straws.

It struck him that after long days of mucking out stalls, wrestling with heavy bales of hay and playing nursemaid to a bunch of animals that did nothing so far as he could tell except eat their fill—not to mention letting out hems on Pete's Sunday pants, hearing his homework and then tackling the paperwork that went along with running even the smallest operation—she needed something more. Something for herself.

He would like to take her out for a night on the town. Dinner, a movie—maybe a bit of dancing. Oh, yeah…with Ellen wearing silk and pearls and him in his borrowed jeans and his ruined shoes.

He'd never even seen Ellen wearing a dress. She'd be a knockout, though. He'd lay odds on that. She was a knockout in baggy jeans, scuffed boots and her husband's old shirts.

Idly, he wondered what kind of frivolous interests she would pursue if she had the time, the freedom and the money. Tennis? Bridge? Shopping sprees? He had an idea it would be more on the order of charity drives and volunteer work.

There was a field full of stubble where hay had recently been cut and baled. Booker and Clyde must have extended themselves at some point in their good-for-nothing lives, because he couldn't see Ellen up on that old tractor.

Or maybe he could. Hell, he didn't know what she was capable of. She kept on surprising him. First with her strength, then with her vulnerability. It was a tricky combination.

"Supper's ready in ten minutes," he announced. "You want to pick up Pete first, or will Ludlum bring him back?"

"I'll get him. I hate to ask the Ludlums to do it. Mr. Ludlum has a handicapped tag, although he seems to get around pretty well. I've never even met Mrs. Ludlum. They keep to themselves."

"Next time you might want to pick nosier neighbors."

"Why, so they'd help us find out who you are and where you belong?"

He was reading the instructions on the back of a box of rice—part two of the three-part meal he was concocting. "So they'd check on you after a disaster to see how you fared. Only common courtesy."

"I told you they called." Ellen placed three plates on the table and grabbed a handful of cutlery. "Storm, why won't you let me see what the library has on amnesia? You could hold back supper and I could go on into town after I pick up Pete."

He rummaged around in a drawer and came up with a set of measuring spoons. "I'm not sure. I guess I thought I'd have snapped out of it by now."

"Or you're afraid of what you might find out," she suggested.

His bleak look said it all. "There you go."

"But what harm could it do just to read about the causes, the possible treatments—maybe the possible duration?"

He shrugged. "Who knows? Maybe amnesia is a means of avoiding something I'm not ready to confront." It was only one of the things he had considered. There were others, each scarier than the last.

The cutlery clattered onto the table. "And maybe that's a big bunch of bologna. You had a knot on your head the size of a turnip. It was physical, not some psycho hoodoo you worked yourself into believing to keep from facing something you're not ready to deal with. If there's one thing I know about you, Storm Hale, or whoever you are, it's that you're not a coward."

"Oh, yeah? Since when did you get to be such an expert? And for your information, my knot was the size of a cantaloupe, not a turnip. Which pan do you use for rice?"

She bent and jerked a stainless-steel pot from under the counter while Storm stared at the ridge of her panties clearly visible under her worn jeans. He could visualize each layer all too clearly—right down to the motherlode.

Damn it, he was no better than that beer-swilling pothead of a hired hand.

Plunking the stainless-steel boiler down on the counter, she said, "This one, the lid fits tight enough. Do you know how to cook rice?"

"Why not ask me something simple, like why the sky's blue?"

"I already know the answer to that one."

He measured out a cup and a half of water, then reached for the box of rice. "Oh, yeah?"

"Dry the cup before you measure the rice, else you'll never get it all out. It's called turbid media." On another woman, her smile would have been called a smirk. On Ellen, it was…a smirk.

"Smarty pants," he muttered, holding the cup up to

eye level to check the measurement. "You're just dying for me to ask what that means, aren't you?"

"No I'm not," she said, all innocence. "I'd better go get Pete before he wears out his welcome."

The chicken and vegetables—more of the latter than the former—was rubbery. He'd forgotten to salt the rice, but it was edible. Pete wasn't hungry. Storm couldn't much blame him. From now on, maybe Ellen should do the cooking.

Along with everything else, he thought guiltily.

She said something. He wasn't paying attention. She tilted her head to stare at him while Pete shoved his supper into a neat pile and compacted it with the fork. "What is it? What's wrong? Are you starting to remember?" she asked.

"I'm not sure," he said slowly. "Almost. I think. Something just popped into my head, but when I tried to grab it, it was gone."

"A name? An S name or an H name? The monogram, remember? How about Storm Harrison? Harrison Storm? Harry Smith?"

"How 'bout Kevin Costner?" Pete offered. "It's got a s and h in it."

"Sorry, partner, no h. Your spelling grade just slipped another notch."

It was like trying to race over a patch of quicksand. No matter how fast you ran, you got sucked down. He remembered once when...

"'Scuse me," he said, raking back his chair.

"Storm?"

"It's okay, I just feel like getting some air. Save the dishes, I'll do 'em later."

She rose and came after him. "You'll do no such

thing. Tell me what's wrong, and don't tell me it's your cooking, it really wasn't all that awful.''

"Damning with a bit of faint praise?" Shoving his arms into Jake's flannel-lined denim coat, he turned toward the door.

Ellen caught him by the hand. "Please, I can't help you if you won't let me. Whatever it is you remembered—almost remembered—tell me and maybe I can make a connection."

"Get the books."

She stepped back, catching her breath. "All right," she said quietly. "I'll go back now. The library doesn't close until nine."

Cold air flowed in through the open front door. In early winter, the days were warm enough, but the temperature plummeted once the sun went down. Storm said, "No, don't go. It'll wait. I'm sorry, I didn't mean to upset you, it's just— It was so close!"

She'd picked up his hand again and was unconsciously rubbing his knuckles. If it was supposed to be soothing, he could have told her it missed by a Texas mile. To hell with his name, right now he was tempted to sweep her into his arms and take her upstairs. Not to the bed he slept in, because that had been her husband's bed those last few weeks before he'd gone to the hospital.

"Sorry if I was a little too dramatic."

"Stop apologizing. I want to help any way I can, but I refuse to fight you for the privilege." She had a way of looking him directly in the eye, but where hers were clear as tourmaline, his had more than once been called inscrutable.

And how in the hell did he know that?

"Listen, don't go to the library tonight." He started

to tell her she could drop him off there tomorrow, or better yet, lend him her truck. Only he didn't have a library card and he didn't have a driver's license. He had a name—Harrison. Maybe.

The phone book was full of Harrisons, a few of them with the right initials. He had called another one today, only to have a woman's voice answer, "Jessica Harrison. I'm unable to come to the phone now, but if you'll leave a message—"

He'd hung up, too discouraged to hear any more. He was increasingly certain he had some connection with the missing district attorney. With that much to go on, it might have made sense to let the police take over his search for an identity, but for some reason he was gut-deep reluctant to do it. That very reluctance seemed to feed on itself, making him even more reluctant. It was almost as if the information was there for the taking, but he was afraid to reach out. Afraid of something, anyway.

Hadn't she as much as accused him of just that? Of being afraid to face reality?

"Ellen, there's something you'd better know. It might be important." Now he was stroking her hand.

From the kitchen Pete yelled, "Mom, I've cleaned off my plate, now can I have seven cookies?"

"Three," she called back without removing her gaze from Storm's face.

"He actually ate that stuff?" Storm queried softly.

"Technicality. He cleaned it off into the garbage can. Pete doesn't lie."

Chuckling, he lowered his chin so that it rested on the top of her head. God, he needed moments like this. Call it respite—call it salvation. She smelled like shampoo and hay and just a bit like horse, but it was a good smell. A wholesome smell.

"What do I need to know?" she prompted, her voice partially muffled in the folds of the shirt he was wearing.

"That I think I might have a reason to avoid cops. I could have turned myself in as soon as I could've made it into town, but for some reason—" He broke off, sweat beading his forehead with the effort to drag forth the information that was so tantalizingly close. "Can you think of one good reason for a man to be afraid of the law? Other than the obvious, that is."

She didn't move. Didn't look up and didn't reply.

"Ellen?"

"I'm working on it." She took a deep breath, then said, "Look, you want to know what I think? I definitely don't think you're a criminal. I'm sure there are any number of perfectly good reasons why someone wouldn't particularly want to get involved with the police."

"Name one," he challenged. She stepped back and his arms fell away. He replaced them and pulled her close again. She might not need it, but he sure as hell did.

"All right, I will. How about if the cops were crooked?"

He took a deep breath and held it. "Are they?"

"Not that I've ever heard. But then, I've never had any reason to find out. Out here in the county we have a sheriff. So far as I know, his department is above reproach."

"So far as you know."

She sighed. He leaned against the wall and pulled

her against him. It seemed the most natural thing in the
world. "So far as I know," she repeated.

"Mind telling me something?"

"Anything. Name, age, weight, childhood nick-
name?" It was a deliberate effort to ease the tension,
they both recognized it as such. Recognized the need
for it, as well.

"None of the above. Although the childhood nick-
name sounds interesting."

"It's not. What else do you want to know?"

"What's a turbid medium?"

She actually laughed aloud at that. Eyes sparkling,
she leaned back against his arms—at least as far as he
would let her—and said, "Art theory. Did I tell you I
studied art in college? Lord knows why, you can't
make a living at it, but at the time, that wasn't a con-
sideration."

"And the meaning is…?" he drawled, smothering
the uncomfortable knowledge that by pursuing trivial
answers he was avoiding more meaningful ones.

"It was a painting technique used by some of the
old masters. Using a thin white wash over a warm
color. The result was cool, sort of like blue without
being actually blue, if you know what I mean."

Slowly, he shook his head. "I'd better write that
down before it gets lost. Never can tell when you might
need to know something like that."

She laughed, and he did, too, and then his face
moved toward hers. The atmosphere was suddenly
fraught. Pending. The way it had been just before the
tornado had come roaring down on him.

The kiss started almost as an experiment. His lips
brushed against hers, caressing gently—moist flesh
dragging softly against moist flesh. It was an incredibly

tender kiss. When the tip of his tongue touched the corner of her mouth, she gripped his shirt with both fists. The heavy jacket he was wearing—her husband's jacket—was suddenly too warm. There were no romantic trappings, none at all, yet never had he been more moved by any woman. By any kiss. Without knowing how he knew, he simply knew.

It was the sound of a breaking dish that tore them apart. Ellen jerked in his arms and blinked up at him, her lips still damp from his kiss. "I'd better—"

"Yeah, me, too."

Seven

Grateful for the distraction, Ellen hurried into the kitchen, followed more slowly by Storm. "Need a hand?" he asked.

"I'm sorry, Mom. It just slipped out of my hand."

"Right. And your supper just slipped into the garbage can." Confronted with the evidence of her son's wasted meal, Ellen was forced to deal with it. She'd been avoiding too many issues for too long, using the excuse that Pete had just lost his father, that she was too tired or too busy. Or both.

There followed a brief lecture—brief because she really was tired and there was still Clyde and Booker and the fence to deal with. After a hug and a promise, Ellen sent Pete to his room with orders not to come downstairs again until he'd done his assigned reading and written the one-page essay for history. "That doesn't mean you can write three words on a line and call it a page," she warned.

"Yes, ma'am." Suitably chastised, the boy trudged upstairs, looking as if he'd lost his last friend.

"I'll be interested in reading it if you get through before my bedtime," Storm called after him. "Your mama makes me go to bed early, though, so don't take too long."

Pete smiled weakly at the joke.

"I'd better ride out before dark to see how far they got with the fence," Ellen said.

"You stay, I'll go."

"Not in my truck, you won't. You don't have a license, remember? Besides, you don't even know where to look."

"Then I'll take one of the horses and you can tell me where to go."

"One of us needs to stay here with Pete."

"You stay. Or come with me if you insist. He's eight years old, Ellen. It's not like we're going to be out until all hours."

"Eight years old is too young to be left alone. Besides, what do you know about children?" She knew she was irritable because she was worried and because she was tired. Knowing the cause, however, was no excuse for rudeness. Storm was only trying to be helpful.

If he truly wanted to be helpful, he would open his arms and let her hide in his embrace until she was ready to face what had to be faced.

Oh, for heaven's sake, Ellen, why not whine? she jeered silently. You're so darned good at it!

In the brief silence that followed Storm said, "About children? At the moment, not much."

She had to think back to recall what she had asked. It was not only rude, it was insensitive. "Sorry."

"No need. Look, if I thought Pete couldn't handle being alone for half an hour, I'd insist you stay here. What if you got into trouble? You could trip over a strand of wire and break a leg, then I'd be stuck here waiting for you to come back. I wouldn't know where to begin to look for you."

"So now it's all about you and your comfort level.

Oh, for goodness' sake, come on, then. It won't take more than a few minutes to drive out and see how far they got.''

Neither of them spoke on the bumpy drive until Ellen said quietly, "I'm sorry, Storm. I'm being even bitchier than usual. It's been one of those days."

He shifted slightly on the bench seat, trying to find a place where a spring didn't poke at his back. He had an idea about what was bothering her most, and it wasn't Pete. Nor was it the fence, which might or might not have been repaired.

It was her father. Whatever had happened between the two of them in the past, Storm suspected she'd told him only a small part of the story. Now, thanks to Sanders's showing up today to remind her of her filial obligation, her conscience was eating at her. He wished to God there was something he could do, but not only was it none of his business, he was in no position at the moment to do anything for anyone, other than the most menial of chores.

It hadn't rained since the day of the twister. A setting sun tinted the dusty air, lending the entire scene an aura of unreality. The air smelled of cattle, citrus fruit and pine trees, not an altogether unpleasant combination.

Ellen swerved into a small clearing just off the dirt road. "We'll pull over here. The broken section is…"

"Still broken," he finished for her. They sat in the truck and stared through the dusty windshield at the broken strands of barbed wire and the leaning fence posts. Long moments passed in silence, then Ellen took a deep breath, opened the door and stepped down.

Storm followed suit, coming around to stand just behind her. His arms reached out instinctively, but at the last moment he hooked his thumbs into the belt loops of his jeans. He had a feeling it wouldn't take much to break that brittle control of hers and that was the last thing she needed now.

On the other hand, maybe a good noisy cry was just what the doctor ordered.

Instead of crying, she used her soft, husky voice to express her thoughts, uttering words she probably hadn't learned in a girl's finishing school. "I'll kill those two miserable bastards, I swear I will. I'll wring their mangy necks until their ears fall off, then I'll fire their lazy, incompetent backsides."

Hastily covering a grin, Storm said solemnly, "I couldn't have put it better myself. First, though, we have to find them."

"Oh, they'll turn up eventually. Where else could they get even minimum wage for doing practically nothing? Friday was payday, so they won't come back until they've drunk up the last penny and slept off a monster hangover. It didn't take me long to catch on. Mondays are usually no-show. Even Tuesdays are iffy—one or the other might make it. From Wednesday 'till Friday afternoon, they get a few jobs done, and that's it. Then they're off on another binge."

The tools were scattered on the ground. More for something to do with his hands than for any other reason, Storm rounded them up and tossed them into the back of the pickup. While he was at it, he tested one of the nearby posts to see how sound it was. The thing slowly toppled, dragging down three rows of rusty barbed wire.

Ellen closed her eyes. Her shoulders drooped. "He was right, I knew he was right. I just didn't want to admit it."

"There's nothing we can do today," Storm said.

"Those grapefruit trees on the other side of the fence aren't going anywhere over the next few hours." At least the creeps hadn't stolen her tools.

They were both still standing beside the truck. "I'll drive," he said gruffly, and it was an indication of her state of mind that she simply nodded. She made no move to get in. Neither did he. In the rapidly fading light, shadows played over her face, emphasizing her cheekbones and the clean line of her brow.

This was crazy, he told himself. His attraction to her. Ellen Wagner—single mother, small-time rancher, tough as old boots, dressed like an upscale scarecrow? So how come he kept picturing her in that old white bathrobe, smelling of shampoo and baby powder, her hair still damp from the shower, looking like every man's favorite's dream?

"I guess we'd better go," he said before his libido overcame his better judgment.

"I guess so," she whispered. It was the hint of a break in her voice that finished him off. Without a second thought, he caught her to him and held her, his face pressing against her hair.

"Ellen, Ellen," he muttered, "What am I going to do about you?"

As the last streak of gold disappeared behind the deep purple clouds, a mourning dove began her soft threnody. Lust mutated into something less tangible, but equally powerful. Eyes closed, Storm allowed his senses to absorb the sounds of the evening, the fragrance of ripening grapefruit and the feel of woman in his arms—her delicate strength and the warm, sweet scent of her hair. He did his best to ignore his body's rising demands because sex was the last thing she needed now.

He only wished there was some way he could adsorb some of her weariness. How long could she go on this way? To what end? Was she fated to grow old trying to hang on to something for a son who might just as easily decide one day to study medicine or law, or maybe join the service like his father had done? There were no guarantees in life. He was a prime example of that fact.

"Let's get you back home, hon." Unconsciously, he used the term of endearment he'd heard her use so often. "You need a good night's sleep."

She sighed. Sighed, but didn't budge an inch. He could feel her breasts pressed against him, feel their soft resilience through the heavy wool shirt she wore. Embarrassed and uncomfortably aroused, he said gruffly, "Let's go."

With a deep, shuddering breath, she turned toward the truck. "Don't look at me," she warned, and so naturally, he looked. Looked and saw the shiny tear tracks wavering down her cheeks.

They rode in silence. He drove. Back at the house she said, "I'd better check things out here before I turn the lights off." She headed for the barn, while Storm, not trusting himself to join her inside the hay-scented, shadow-filled interior, veered toward the house.

"I'll look in on Pete," he said, waiting until she'd switched on the barn lights.

They'd been gone no more than half an hour. Everything looked the same as when they'd left, only darker. He let himself inside and headed upstairs, feeling the familiar comfort of the shabby old farmhouse close around him. He didn't know what he was used to, but he would willingly settle for this. Oh, yeah.

The kid was belly-down, sprawled in a four-point

position, the quilt dragging onto the floor. Storm took a moment to glance around, smiling at the boyish attempt at policing the area. About a week's worth of clothes was neatly heaped on a chair. Schoolbooks, a globe and a dictionary had been shoved to the very edge of the student desk to make room for another plastic F-18 Delta Wing, still under construction. Whether the homework in question had been finished or not remained to be seen.

He couldn't help but smile at an eight-year-old boy's version of housecleaning. Scrape a section of rug bare and pile everything up on the periphery. He had a feeling Ellen would let him get away with it only so long, and then she'd come down on him like a swarm of locusts. Oh, yeah, he knew about little boys.

Because he'd been one, or because he had one?

He didn't even know what to hope for. If he had a son of his own, he could help him with his model planes, tell him what it was like to sit in the cockpit, to see his gloved hand on the stick, to feel the thrust of all that harnessed power—

Standing stock-still, he waited for the picture to come into sharp focus. Instead, it faded out as quickly as it had appeared.

J. S. Harrison. Again he was struck by the coincidence surrounding the disappearance of a man named J. S. Harrison and the appearance of a man with no name, but with a handkerchief bearing two of the three initials. The name could be his—probably was, in fact—but until he could make it fit, there was no point in staking a claim. Especially when he kept having these vague feelings of some nebulous threat hanging over him.

After a moment he pulled the quilt up over Pete's

thin shoulders, ignoring the comic books that got covered up in the process, and tiptoed from the room.

By the time he reached the kitchen, Ellen had come in from the barn. "All secure?" he asked.

"All secure. Is Pete asleep yet?"

"Out like a light." He toyed with a calico potholder shaped like a cow. "You know, I could almost swear I knew something about fighter jets."

"Maybe you collected model planes as a boy." She was reheating the coffee and getting out plates and forks.

"Not F-18s. At least I don't think so. But if I'm military, why wasn't I in uniform?"

"How do I know? Maybe you're an airline pilot. Maybe you opened the door at the wrong time and got sucked out of the plane." She opened the freezer door and stared at the contents, not looking at him. "Hmm. Coconut cake from the freezer or store-bought apple pie?"

"Uh, either. Both?"

"In your dreams."

He watched her neat movements. There was nothing at all seductive in the way she moved or the way she dressed. Yet just watching her was enough to make him forget all but the most basic urges. She had to have noticed. The jeans he was wearing were large, but not that large.

While she set about dividing the pie into even segments, he began to pace in a tight circle, forcing his mind back on track. "You know, it's these little things that keep driving me crazy. I let my guard down and first thing you know, here comes another glimmer. I try to grab hold, and it disappears, like trying to hold on to a handful of fog. I ask you, is that normal?" He uttered a bark of laughter and answered his own question. "Oh, sure. Crazy is normal. Not being sure of your own name, that's normal. Sponging off a woman you never laid eyes on before in your life, that's perfectly normal."

"Sit down."

"Listen, the sooner I get those books and read up on—"

"Sit down and eat. The only thing you're doing now is stirring up dust and wearing out my vinyl floor."

"Tell me again about the guys who came looking for me, Ellen."

"I told you everything I know."

"Tell me again. Something might click."

"Then sit down and eat your dessert. With enough sugar in your bloodstream, maybe you won't go off on a rampage."

"I never indulge in rampages," he informed her, all injured dignity. But he sat, all the same. He picked up his fork, then put it back down. "At least I don't think I do. Describe this pair again. Maybe this time something will ring a bell."

"All right, stop me when you've had enough. There were two of them, as I said before." She took a deep breath. "It was late and I was tired. I think the term is stressed out."

"Go on." Storm tried to harness the frustration that was never far from the surface.

"You know how you keep getting these glimmers? These…I guess they're sort of like hunches?"

"We're talking about you now, not me and my glimmers."

"Yes, well, as I told you before, I had one. And I'm sorry as I can be if I was wrong, but something about those two men just struck me the wrong way. Well, for one thing, I'm almost sure they were lying. I mean, if they were looking for a friend, wouldn't they have been more distraught? Concerned, at the very least?''

''I take it they weren't. These two cool dudes identified me as their buddy, J. S. Harrison? I probably am, you know. Harrison, if not their buddy.''

''Oh, for goodness' sake, do you honestly think I'd have kept you here if you were that kind of person? I couldn't even bear to have them on my property, much less in my house.''

''Describe them.''

She shrugged. ''Like I said before, one of them didn't say anything—he was short, actually, not much bigger than I am. I couldn't tell about his features, he had this hat on. The other one had all the tattoos. He was wearing a black T-shirt, but parts of his tattoos showed above his neckline—either flames or snakes...or maybe they were octopus tentacles, I don't know. I'm no expert on tattoo designs.''

Storm mentally examined two separate parts of the puzzle: the two lowlifes who for some reason were trying to track him down and the nebulous link with a missing district attorney. How did they fit together? Or did they? He stared morosely at the untouched pie. It appeared increasingly likely that the nagging sense of connection with jails and prisons wasn't so far-fetched after all.

What about his instinctive reluctance to go to the cops? Where did that fit in? Was it another part of the puzzle or totally unrelated?

''I seem to have lost my appetite,'' he said quietly.

Ellen looked close to tears, and he forced himself to shove his own problems back under cover. They both

knew she should have told him as soon as the two
goons had showed up, but making her feel guilty now
wasn't going to solve his problems. Sooner or later
another piece of the puzzle would come into focus, and
he'd be on his way to solving the riddle.

Her own problems, he suspected, would not be
solved that easily, and that troubled him almost as
much as his own situation did. But at least he could
spare her the burden of guilt.

"For what it's worth, Ellen, I think you did the right
thing. At the time, I was in no position to defend myself." *Or you.* The words popped into his mind unbid-
den, and he accepted the fact that until he knew exactly
what the situation was, and where any possible danger
might conceivably come from, she was potentially as
vulnerable as he was.

Her lips trembled. He didn't know if she was about
to cry or to smile. He did know she tempted him beyond belief. He picked up his fork again. "This pie
looks delicious," he said with forced cheerfulness.
"You say you bought it with your own lily-white
hands?"

"Oh, hush up," she muttered, sliding her own plate
closer.

Some ten minutes later they parted friends. Or if not
exactly friends, certainly not enemies. He told her that
while she'd make a damned fine witness with her eye
for detail, he wasn't certain instinct was admissible in
court.

"Who knows, maybe you saved me from having a
warrant served on me. Could be they were bail bonds-
men or bounty hunters. I might have been on my way
to the border when fate in the form of that twister intervened."

She yawned, then said something about Pete and guardian angels, but distracted as he was by the tempting shadows that followed the line of her throat, he missed most of it.

He had a feeling sleep wouldn't come easily tonight. "As much as I hate to eat and run, one of us, mentioning no names, is bushed. How about we save the dishes until tomorrow, and I'll wash them with the breakfast things."

"You're spoiling me."

"I hope so. Someone damned well should," he said gruffly. And like the fool he was, he stood and reached for her hand just as she got to her feet. What the devil was this magnetic attraction between them? Did she feel it, too, or was she only tired—tired and maybe feeling sorry for him?

Wrapping his arms around her, he gave her a final squeeze, resisting the temptation to kiss her senseless. "Go to bed. I'll lock up and turn off the lights."

Hours later he lay awake, staring into the darkness, his mind off again on the trail of his missing identity. Given a choice of several options, he would prefer to be the missing D.A., but there was an equally good chance that he was some kind of white-collar crook. A crime boss. The well-dressed type that moved easily among certain levels of the political and business community. The concept didn't exactly feel…alien.

Oh, hell, he was probably just a traveling salesman with a talent for self-dramatization.

Think, damn it, think! It was there—so close. So tantalizingly close. It was almost as if he didn't want to remember….

Forcing himself to concentrate on the shadows cast by the night-light, he eventually dozed.

And awoke at daybreak, knowing.

Knowing!

Eight

His first impulse was to leap out of bed to go find Ellen. He had actually reached for his clothes—he'd long since quit sleeping in her husband's pajamas—when he stopped dead in his tracks.

The story about the missing D.A. had run only twice to his knowledge. Why had it been dropped? He might not be important as a man, but his position was important. Damned important, especially right now when the mob was in a desperate fight for more influence over Mission Creek politics.

That last headline—Newly Appointed D.A. To Continue Prosecution In Judge's Murder Case—hadn't made any sense. Del Brio had to be behind the new appointment. It had to have been Del Brio who'd applied pressure where it would do the most good. Otherwise they'd have held up the trial and put out an all-points.

No wonder the story in the *Mission Creek Clarion* had made him feel like throwing up. His belly had been trying to tell his brain to hurry up and get back to town before Black could be railroaded by a corrupt newly appointed D.A. He'd needed to get back in time to make a deal with Black, who'd been delegated to take the fall, to trade his testimony for a reduced sentence.

Taking several deep breaths, Spence confronted himself, vital statistics, flaws and all. Jason Spencer Harrison, age 35, born in Midland, Texas, no stranger to juvenile court before he'd been hauled up before a tough judge named Carl Bridges. It had been that same judge who had jerked him up by the collar—figuratively, if not quite literally. Judge Bridges had set him on a track that had led eventually to Virginia Military Institute, the marine corps—hell, he even had a Silver Star in his dresser drawer. And a law career.

Feeling as if he were on a fast-moving roller-coaster car with no safety bar, Spence attempted to assimilate all the data to figure out what must have taken place behind the scenes after he'd dropped out of sight. Not all of it would have made the evening news. Even the parts that did would have been subjected to a hell of a lot of spin. Such as his disappearance. What had they done, put out the word that he'd dropped out in the middle of a trial he was preparing to prosecute to pay a lengthy visit to his great-aunt in Rhode Island?

He didn't have a great-aunt in Rhode Island or anywhere else. Didn't have any relatives at all, as far as he knew. Remembering a few incidents from his so-called formative years, it was just as well.

Damn it, if he knew who was doing the spinning, he might be able to figure out which way to jump. Part of the trouble was that there were too many shades of gray in a town like Mission Creek, where the same families had been interacting for generations. He could count on one hand the number of guys he knew for sure he could trust with his life. A few more that he could probably trust, but in this case, "probably" wasn't good enough. Something heavy was going down, and until he knew what it was and who was involved, directly and indirectly, he'd do well to remain out of sight.

Across the hall in the living room, the mantel clock announced 4:00 a.m. Spence fought down the urge to race to the kitchen, grab the phone and start dialing, regardless of the time. Luke was probably still out of touch, somewhere in Central America trying to locate Phillip Westin to bring him out. God knew they owed the man. As leader of their Special Forces team, Westin had risked his neck to rescue them after they'd been taken captive and held under...shall we say, less than hospitable circumstances, Spence reminisced with a bitter smile.

They had survived that. He could survive this. Flynt and Tyler should still be in town. Why hadn't they put out an all-points on him? They had to have known when he hadn't showed up to take that deposition that something was wrong. The twister had cut directly across his route, whether he'd been traveling on the interstate or through farm country. The fact that they hadn't made a move indicated that they'd had a good reason not to.

Lying flat on his back, one arm under his head, the other hand idly tracing a scar on his shoulder, a memento from his days in captivity, Spence began sifting through the known data. Knowing—or at least guessing at the who, what, where and when was a starting place. It was the why that really screwed up the works. And there was no way of determining the why without more evidence.

By the time he fell asleep he had made up his mind not to reveal his recovered memory to anyone. What he'd seen on the news and read in the papers might or might not be true. Either way, it was far from the whole story. If Ellen knew, he'd have no further excuse to stay, and until he found out which way the wind blew, it was imperative that he stay underground. He'd been playing hardball with some pretty rough characters when he'd dropped out of sight. He didn't want her involved.

His first impulse had been to call either Flynt or Tyler, but phone calls were traceable. He'd have to think that one over. Hell, maybe he'd write a letter. No return address, of course. After all this time, another few days wouldn't matter. He could follow the court news from here, and if it looked as if Black's trial was going to be rushed to conclusion, he could always show up and put a spoke in the wheels of injustice. Granted, Alex Black was a hired gun. Granted, he deserved to serve maximum time. But the man who had ordered the hit was Spence's real target. Until that man was accounted for, it would be business as usual for the drug czars and pseudo-respectable money-launderers.

Waking later than usual that morning, Spence lay in bed, deliberately going over all the pertinent data. By the time he showered, shaved, dressed and made it to the kitchen, Ellen and Pete had already had breakfast and left.

Glancing out the window, he watched Pete empty the wheelbarrow and head back inside the barn just as Ellen led the two mares out to the paddock. Which meant it was Saturday again. Either that, or one of those vague holidays teachers used to catch up on red-tape regulations.

Up until today the calendar had been largely meaningless, marking off, as it did, his term of suspended animation. That was how he'd eventually come to think of his situation. He'd been alive. Oh, yeah, he'd been that, all right. Alive in ways that were becoming increasingly awkward under the circumstances. Until now there'd been no way of knowing whether his sex life had suffered from a long, dry spell, or whether two weeks of abstinence had pushed his limit.

He was beginning to suspect that the answer was neither. The answer could be stated simply in one word.

Ellen.

And that was another problem that would have to be dealt with. Ellen and Pete. Whatever happened, they were going to be a part of his life in one capacity or another, if he had anything to say about it. Any possible relationship would have to be put on hold. The sooner he got this mess straightened out, the sooner he could concentrate on sorting out his personal life.

Ellen was leading the stallion out by the time he joined her. Pete had already started to muck out Zeus's stall. One of the barn cats raced past and the big bay kicked out, knocking over a bucket. Ellen took a tighter grip on the lead. "What this guy needs is a long, hard ride to work off some energy, only I'm not sure I'm up to it. Clyde's been up on him a time or two, but I didn't much like the way he handled him."

Spence moved to lean on the fence beside her, admiring the big bay horse. "Want me to give him a run?"

She tilted her head to study him under the broad brim of her battered straw Resistol. "Do you think you could manage him?"

He started to say he'd ridden bigger, meaner horses before he was much older than Pete, but changed it to, "We won't know until I try, will we?"

"Maybe you'd better start out on one of the others. The geldings are gentle. The mares, too, only they probably shouldn't be ridden at this late stage. Which reminds me, I'd better call the vet. I think it's getting close to time. With horses, the term evidently varies.'' Curling a sidelong smile at him, she added, ''My To Do list is growing like Pinocchio's nose.''

She wasn't complaining, merely stating a fact, but it occurred to Spence that she was right. It all added up to more than one woman and a kid could handle. As long as he was still here, he could sure as hell exercise the horses for her. He was no rodeo star, but he hadn't been thrown in years.

Of course, he hadn't ridden all that much in years, either, and breaking his neck on a half-raw stallion wouldn't help matters at this point. At the moment, however, he had other priorities. Zeus would have to take a number and wait.

''Pete, help me tack up the geldings, will you?'' Spence called.

''We going to ride?'' the boy asked excitedly.

''Either you and me or your mamma and me. I need to—'' He'd been going to say he needed to loosen up a few riding muscles before he tackled the stallion. Again he changed course at the last moment. Lying, either by omission or by diversion, was still lying. He didn't like doing it, but until he was ready to tell the whole truth, it was the best he could do. ''I need to find out if I know anything about these critters, and your mama says the mares probably shouldn't be ridden.''

''Clyde, he rides Miss Sara all the time,'' the boy said.

Ellen snorted. ''Oh, shoot! I told him plainly that they weren't to ride either of the mares. There's no need. That's what the geldings are for.''

Spence laid a hand on Ellen's arm. ''Shh, don't

bother. The ladies look okay to me and your two creeps are not around to take their punishment. Save the pyrotechnics for when they'll do some good.''

"Fat chance of that. I doubt if Clyde and Booker will show their faces around here anytime soon.''

"Good riddance.'' Spence saddled Sam, the larger of the two geldings, while Pete fastened the cinch on the other one.

Then the boy shoved his small hand into a worn, man-size work glove. "Mama, you go first, okay? I've got to finish mucking out, then Storm and me'll ride.''

Ellen's eyes met Spence's over the gelding's rump. Hers were questioning, his amused. He had a pretty good idea what the kid was up to. Pete was smart enough to know his mama needed a dependable man around. Evidently, he'd just been elected.

He wondered if Ellen had any inkling.

Evidently not. She said, "Pete loves riding almost as much as he dislikes mucking out stalls. Maybe I'd better stay here and send him out with you.''

"No way, lady. If I take a fall, I want someone around who's big enough to get me on my feet again. You've had experience, remember?'' Grinning, Spence waited until the boy had gone back inside. "Besides, it wouldn't do any good. Your son's matchmaking, Mama. Don't you know anything?''

"Oh, for goodness' sake, that's absurd!'' She hooked a booted foot in the stirrup and swung aboard, graceful as any ballerina despite her baggy work clothes.

Spence mounted and said, "On the other hand, a kid sees his mother struggling to make a go of a place like this, knows there's only so much he can do for the next few years and it's not enough, knows how hard good help is to come by. What's the next logical step?''

"I don't know. There isn't one," she snapped. Then, impatiently, "Oh, don't be so ridiculous!"

They rode out of the yard and headed down the long back lane. Ellen took the lead, her back rigid. She muttered something that sounded like, "You think you're so smart, don't you?" He thought she was blushing, but under the shade of her hat brim, he couldn't be sure.

Grinning, he called after her, "Marginally smarter than I was yesterday." Let her figure that out. He still hadn't decided what, if anything, to tell her. He felt like a cur for deceiving her, but the fewer people who knew he was still alive, the better. Until he got a handle on what was going on in town.

At the time he'd dropped out of sight, Westin's disappearance and Black's trial weren't all that was happening. There'd been an ongoing tug-of-war between Frank Del Brio and Ricky Mercado over which one would take over as mob boss. Spence hadn't liked the idea of it being Mercado, a former friend and comrade in spite of his family's mob involvement. The alienation that had occurred when Spence, Flynt and Tyler had been implicated in the disappearance of Ricky's sister had never really dissipated. They'd been cleared, of course, thanks to Judge Bridges, but the constraint was still there.

On the other hand, Spence knew that with Ricky in place as mob boss, they might be able to work together to scale things back before everything blew wide open. There was a lot of good stuff in Ricky Mercado.

There was a lot of money in Lone Star County, too, and a lot of generations-old ties. Where there was money, there was crime. Where there were old ties, trouble usually simmered just beneath the surface. All Spence had hoped to accomplish as district attorney was to keep things under some sort of control by weeding out the worst elements.

He now knew the identity of the two men who'd come looking for him. Knew them by reputation, if not personally. Peaches and Silent Sal were Del Brio's men, about as low as it got in that particular pecking order. They might as well wear sandwich boards to advertise their profession. If Del Brio had wanted to find him, he should have sent a more convincing emissary. If he'd wanted to make sure he stayed dead, that pair would have done the job just fine.

Which was a pretty good indication of which way the wind was blowing.

Ellen eased her mount from a brisk trot to a walk, her back no longer looking as if she had a ramrod for a spine. All around them the smells of a south Texas autumn were in the air. Dust. Grapefruit. Freshly manured fields. Someone was burning stumps, the pungent smoke drifting for miles on the warming air. The only sound to be heard was the occasional call of a bobwhite.

Peaceful. A man could live a full, productive life out here in the open country and never miss the fast lane.

Spence moved easily with the gait of the big sorrel. If Ellen noticed, she didn't mention it. Instead, when he caught up with her, she said with no preamble, "He wouldn't match-make, you know. Pete adored his father, he wouldn't want any man—"

It took him a minute to work his way back to their conversation. "Ellen, your son might not be a whiz at spelling, but look at the way he handles things around here. Most kids would bitch and groan at having to do chores before school, after school and on weekends. He pitches in like a real trouper. I've yet to hear him complain.''

''Is that what your children are like? Whining at being asked to do a few chores? If so, blame the parent, not the child.''

What could he say? ''I don't have a son, don't have a wife, don't even have a significant other.'' Not without explaining how he knew, and he wasn't yet ready to do that.

Actually, what he had was a comfortable arrangement with a lady sales rep for a Napa Valley winery. Cassie was single, of sound mind and spectacular body. The sex was great on the rare occasions when she was in town and they were both free, usually about every six weeks or so.

They rode in silence for a while. Overhead, a hawk circled lazily. Applying the slightest pressure with his heels, Spence urged the gelding into a gallop, as if trying to outdistance any further leading questions.

Ellen caught up with him when he reached the fallen fence post. ''I'm sorry, Storm. I shouldn't take my frustrations out on you.''

Dismounting, he ground-tied his mount and looked around. ''I don't suppose you've got a supply of new posts handy?''

''There were some locust posts in the loft when we bought the place. Six or seven. As far as I know, they're still there.''

Scanning the fence line, Storm said judiciously, ''It would barely be a start, but if we replaced about every third post that should get us as far as the corner. The bracing looks pretty solid. Is that yours?'' He indicated the grove of grapefruit trees in the distance.

''Technically, yes. It's one of the sections I lease out. I don't know anything at all about growing citrus fruit, and Jake wasn't particularly interested. All he wanted to do was raise horses.''

''At least you've got a start on that. Pretty soon you'll have increased your herd.''

''Yes, well, that happened sort of accidentally, too. The man who sold them to us said to wait at least a year before breeding the mares. By the time the year was up, Jake had already been diagnosed. The prognosis wasn't…well, suffice to say, the horses were the last thing on my mind. Later on, Mr. Caster said we'd better either breed the mares or get rid of Zeus before he kicked the place down, so I told him to go ahead with the breeding. Speaking of fence repairs, that's why I'm short of supplies. That darned Zeus. And according to the vet, the mares will be ready again less than two weeks after they drop a foal. Honestly, I'm not sure if I can handle this job.''

Spence was tempted to tell her she had no business even trying to run a breeding operation when she didn't know the first thing about it. But he knew why she was doing it, and he couldn't argue with her sentiments. As he saw it, she had damned few options. Sell out and use the money to relocate to someplace where the job market was better than it was around here and where the schools were just as good. But with no special training, what kind of a job could she find that would support the two of them?

Her other option was going home to Daddy. He had a feeling that wasn't going to happen anytime soon. If she went back at all it would be at a time when she didn't need the old man's help.

The cold front that had ushered in the rash of severe weather had long since moved out. Today it was muggy, but not at all unpleasant. He rolled back the sleeves of his borrowed shirt while Ellen removed the leather vest she'd been wearing and hung it over the saddle.

"How good are you at fencing?" she asked, then before he could answer, she shook her head, laughing. "Don't bother to answer. You don't know, right?"

Oh, boy. Talk about weaving a tangled web. "Are we talking foils and sabers here?"

"We're talking post-hole diggers, wire-pullers and staples."

One thing he was good at was avoiding direct answers. It was a lawyer's stock in trade. They argued briefly about the merits of stringing new wire, which she didn't have enough of on hand, as opposed to re-fastening the old wire to new posts. He told her truthfully that she knew more about fencing than he did.

Spence knew his way around a ranch, up to a point. He knew how to use tools, up to that same point. He'd worked his way through college doing everything from wrangling to managing a car wash. "How good a fence do you need to separate a herd of grapefruit trees from a dirt road?" he asked on the ride back.

"Very funny. Ever hear the saying, good fences make good neighbors?"

"So that explains why none of your neighbors came to check on you after the tornado. Your fence was down."

"I didn't need any checking, if you'll remember.

Besides, I had you. Pete told Mr. Ludlum that we had someone staying with us to help out.''

And Ludlum had told how many others? That was a potential problem. Evidently Del Brio's men had had some idea of where to start looking. They wanted him dead, not alive. If word leaked out that he was still alive and the same guys turned up again, they'd be armed. Probably had been the first time. He'd like to think he could handle it, but he had to be sure before he put Ellen and Pete in any danger. Yesterday or any time during the past two weeks, he'd have been a sitting duck.

What the devil had happened to his car? Not to mention the things that had been in it? Maybe the best thing he could do would be to get out of here, suddenly show up in town and let the chips start flying, but if he left now, Ellen and Pete would be vulnerable and he wouldn't be there to protect them. Del Brio wasn't dumb. He was hotheaded, but he wasn't stupid. He would much rather have him out of the picture permanently, but barring that, he would know just where and how to apply pressure to make sure Spence took early retirement and moved out of the area. And for the time being, Ellen and Pete were his Achilles' heel.

Bottom line, now that Del Brio had his own man in place as D.A., the last thing the new mob boss wanted was to have the real one turn up, especially in the middle of Alex Black's trial.

Trial, hell, it was going to be a railroad job.

"This is nice," Ellen said softly. So softly he almost missed her words.

He nodded. It occurred to him as they walked the two mounts back along the service road that they might have been friends for years instead of having known each other barely two weeks. It was an easy relationship, far easier in some ways than he'd have expected under the circumstances.

Far more troublesome in others. For one thing he had to stop thinking of her as anything more than a casual acquaintance. It wasn't fair to either of them, not when he'd left so much unfinished business behind.

He told himself that he didn't love Ellen. He liked her a lot—more all the time—but that wasn't love. Lust was something else entirely. Call it a chemical reaction—if so, it was a pretty volatile one. Ellen was a beautiful woman, sexy without making a big deal out of it—strong without being any less feminine. But just because he liked her, just because he wanted to take her to bed, didn't mean he was in love with her.

God, the last thing he needed now was one more complication. If he had to fall in love—and that had been the last thing on his mind when he'd locked his office door and set out to take that deposition two weeks ago—he'd have to find a way to work it into his schedule. Priority one was finding out who had ordered Judge Bridges's murder and seeing that he paid the price. About a hundred and fifty years of hard labor might do it, although he'd settle for sixty.

Along with that situation there was Luke and the commander, both out of contact somewhere in Central America at last report.

Like war, the Texas Mafia was an ongoing problem that no one man was going to be able to put an end to. It was too entrenched, too entangled for too many generations in Lone Star County. The justice system might curtail some of the more egregious activities, but the best the white-hats could hope for was to peel off layers until the whole mess shrunk to a more manageable size.

Frankie Del Brio's slice of the pie was only one small sliver of a vast network that knew no boundaries, local, state, national or otherwise. Anyone who had been on the other side as long as Spence had been knew that eradication was not a possibility; containment and control was the most they could hope for, human nature being what it was.

Nine

"Pete and I can tackle the fence this afternoon," Spence told Ellen, glad to turn his thoughts to a problem more easily solved. "I'll get the posts down from the loft."

"They weigh a ton. Mr. Caster said the reason locust wears like iron is that it weighs almost as much. Something to do with the density. You can shift some stuff up there and roll them out through the hay door."

"Or rig a block and tackle. I saw one hanging out under the shed."

"Jake used it to help remove the power take-off from the tractor."

"Yeah, Pete told me. Ellen, you're going to have to hire some decent help."

"Sure, I'll just put an ad in the paper. 'Hardworking ranch hand needed, minimum wage, no benefits. No binge drinkers or pot smokers need apply.'"

"I'd say that pretty well excludes Clyde and Booker. You knew about the pot?"

"I suspected. Did you?"

"Smelled something the other day that made me wonder. It wasn't tobacco, that I do know."

They rode the last few hundred yards in silence. Spence didn't know the details of her financial situation other than that it had to be pretty bare bones. If she could have afforded better help, she'd have found it.

Yet, her background had been comfortable if not actually affluent. If her father could afford a big fancy wedding, he could certainly afford to see that his daughter didn't have to do the work of two men.

"Any chance your family could find you some decent help?" he asked, knowing in advance what the answer would be. Why couldn't the woman drop her pride just long enough for this mess to blow over? Now Spence was going to have to find her a bodyguard who knew his way around a stable and pass him off as a ranch hand, because he sure as hell wasn't going to go off and leave her here alone. "Ellen? As long as you're mending fences, this might be a good time to pay a visit to your father."

"Forget it." By then they had reached the barn. As if to underscore her self-sufficiency, Ellen slid down off the horse before he could dismount and come around to help her. "We had a housekeeper once who used to mangle metaphors. Whenever I'd blow my allowance and try to talk her into lending me some from the grocery money she'd say, 'You buttered your bread, missy, now you can just lie in it.'"

Reluctantly, Spence conceded defeat. For now. "How does it feel, wallowing in butter?"

"Slippery," she said with a quirky half smile.

Slippery didn't begin to describe it. Damn it, he didn't want to frighten her, but he had to find some way to put her on guard. With any luck he should be able to wind things up PDQ once he got back in action. It was the timing that worried him. The longer he stayed missing, the more confident Del Brio would be, and an overconfident hothead just might get careless. Spence didn't need much more before he wrapped up all the evidence in his possession and handed it over to the feds, leaving them to connect the dots. He'd counted on that deposition, but even without it the evidence was pretty damning.

Meanwhile, it suited him fine to let Del Brio believe he'd been sucked up by that twister and dropped off somewhere in the middle of the Gulf of Mexico.

He unsaddled the horse, rubbed him down and turned him into the paddock. Pete came racing out from the house. "Hey, I thought you guys were going to stay all day. Can I go now? Storm, why'd you unsaddle him? I thought we were going to ride out after you and Mom got back."

"We are, only first we've got us a project."

Lunch was ready by the time Spence and Pete got the block and tackle in position to swing the heavy fence posts down from the loft into the back of the truck. They decided to eat first, then ride out to the work site.

"Wonder why they put 'em up there," Pete said.

"Probably because they weren't needed, but they're too good to throw away. Or maybe to make room for a couple more stalls down below. Any more questions?" Spence ruffled the boy's hair.

"Wonder how they got 'em up there," Pete asked a few minutes later as the two of them were washing up together downstairs.

"Same way we're going to get 'em down." Spence had already explained why rolling the cumbersome eight-foot locust posts out of the loft onto the ground below would not be a good idea, as they would have to be handled again to get them into the truck. Then he'd had to explain what a hernia was.

"Man, you know a bunch of stuff. You know how puppies get made?"

Oh, jeez, I'm not sure I'm up to this, Spence thought ruefully. "I bet your mama could tell you."

"I already know. I was just wondering if you did."

Lunch was baked beans from a can and hot dogs. Pete said, "Cool!"

Spence held Ellen's chair before seating himself. Briefly, they discussed the project while they ate, and Ellen mentioned the two pickups that were parked out beside the tractor shed. "I usually drive the small truck except when I'm pulling the trailer."

"My mom can back up and everything with a trailer," Pete said, his mouth full of hot dog, mustard and bread. "She hardly ever knocks anything down anymore."

Spence winked at Ellen. "We loaded the logs into the duelly," he told her. "I figured you might need to run into town before we got back." It had been agreed that there was no reason he shouldn't drive as long as he stayed on Wagner property. "We should be back before dark."

It had been a few years since he'd driven a stick shift, but the big diesel purred like a kitten under his hands.

Pete brought up the subject of puppies again as they bounced along the rutted lane to the back section. Spence listened with a part of his mind, another part involved in how best to handle the situation in which he found himself. He knew he didn't want to leave Ellen and the boy here alone, and was somewhat surprised to realize that he didn't want to leave them at all. But he had some unfinished business to wind up.

The sooner he took care of that, the better for all concerned. Which, unfortunately, included Pete and Ellen.

His timing would have to be flawless. If Del Brio and his puppet got wind of his reappearance before Spence was ready, the prosecution could rush things to conclusion. Black's court-appointed attorney was barely adequate. Joe Ed Malone had managed to see to that.

On the other hand, arranging for a postponement might not be that easy unless he could come up with a damned good excuse, such as irrefutable evidence of witness tampering. It all depended on how deep Del Brio had managed to burrow into the justice system. A retrial, if it came to that, would take days, probably weeks, at best. Meanwhile, accidents could happen. Jail cell suicides were not unheard of. Case closed.

Damn, he had to get back into action. ''Hand me that post-hole digger, son.''

He grunted and dug, stopping now and then to mop the sweat from his face. Pete, frowning in concentration, pried rusted heavy-duty staples from the rotten wood, agilely avoiding the coils of rusted barbed wire as they sprang free.

Moving down the line, Spence tested the standing posts. All needed replacing, but he had replacements for only a few. You couldn't always tell from looking at a post whether or not it was rotten below the surface.

Not unlike the situation he faced in other areas. In a town like Mission Creek, the good-old-boy brotherhood stretched across too many boundaries, too many generations, making for entirely too many dubious relationships. For what he was about to tackle, he needed a tight cadre of white-hats. With Luke off on another mission, that meant he had to depend on Flynt and

Tyler. If they happened to be out of town, too, he was on his own until he could get the feds involved and bring them up to speed.

Pete came up behind him, dropped the crowbar, whistled and mopped his brow, mimicking Spence's actions. The two stood there, feet spread apart, and studied the progress they'd made.

"He wouldn't have to sleep with me all the time," Pete said gravely. "But it would be sort of nice until he got used to us. I mean, so he wouldn't get lonesome or anything. Don't you think so?"

Back to the present. Spence made the mental adjustment instantaneously. The boy obviously wanted a dog, and just as obviously wanted an ally when he broached the subject with his mother.

"I don't see anything wrong with that—except maybe he should have his own bed in your room instead of sleeping on your bed, in case he rolled in something. Dogs do that occasionally."

"I know." Pete nodded sagely. "Mr. Caster said it was so their enemies couldn't smell 'em. Dogs don't bathe as much as cats do."

"I believe you're right."

Working together, they managed to get five of the seven posts set. It had taken longer than Spence had anticipated, as the ground was rock-hard. Rather than rework the rusted barbed wire in the fading daylight, they decided to wait until morning.

"Cats are okay, only the barn cats are wild." Pete picked up the threads of the earlier conversation once they were in the pickup. "Mom says they have fleas, even the kittens, and if I bring one in the house, the fleas will fall off and get on us, and she doesn't like to use poison sprays."

"Tough. Some moms are like that, though."

Spence downshifted to negotiate a deeply rutted stretch of road. Even bone-tired, he took great pleasure in the smooth coordination of foot on clutch, hand on gearshift. After two weeks of inactivity, he'd jumped at even the most menial jobs. Handling the eight-foot locust fence posts was a good physical workout. Oddly enough, it sharpened his mental faculties, as well, which was probably a good thing. He would need to be in top form when he made his public reappearance.

"Mom says we have to have barn cats, but the last dog we had chased 'em. Then Zeus kicked the dog and he died. He was a real good dog. He ate vegetables, and Mom even let him sleep at the foot of my bed when I had the flu. I keep asking her for another one, but she always says, 'We'll see.' That either means no or wait for Christmas, but this Christmas she's going to get me another bike. See, insurance doesn't cover bikes, I asked Mr. Ludlum. It covers cars and that kind of stuff, but not bikes. So maybe you could talk to her? We pro'ly need a good watchdog, anyway, and I don't care what kind he is. If we get a puppy I can train him to eat vegetables and bark at strangers and all. And not chase cats—only I think dogs have to do that, don't you?"

"Whew! Take a breath, son. We don't have to settle it tonight."

Although, maybe they should. Spence didn't know how much time he had left. Now that he'd managed to win the boy's approval, he was having a few second thoughts. He wasn't sure Pete would understand if he suddenly took off, and he wasn't sure how much he could afford to explain.

"'Kay." Pete took several breaths. As they neared

the house, he glanced around, his hazel eyes large and curious. "What does it feel like?"

"What does what feel like?"

"Not knowing anything. Um, magnesia."

Spence parked the truck beside the horse barn. His gaze automatically scanned the area, looking for something—anything—out of order. Funny, the way his old Special Forces training kicked in after all these years. "Amnesia? It's kind of hard to explain. How about if you went upstairs and opened your bedroom door but didn't turn on the light. You'd know everything was still there, even if you couldn't see it. No," he said after a slight pause. "Bad analogy."

"What a 'nalogy?"

They sat there in the truck, bone-tired, but basking in the satisfaction of having accomplished more than either of them had expected. Spence tried to explain. The boy was like a sponge. An intelligent sponge, but by the time they climbed down to go inside for supper, he wasn't sure which was more exhausted—his brain or his shoulders.

After supper he fixed the leaky kitchen faucet. No big deal, even though he'd never done it before. With all the odd jobs he'd held as a youth—licit and illicit— plumbing was one he'd missed. Ellen handed him the tools and supplies, and logic did the rest. Next, the horses were brought in for the night, rubbed down and fed. Spence helped. He'd worked with horses before, but it had been a while. Over the past couple of years he'd probably managed to spend a total of one week at his own ranch. Thank God for his manager, who treated both stock and property as his own.

"At the rate you're learning, even if you never regained your memory, you could probably get a job as a ranch hand.''

"I'll keep it in mind." As long as it was her ranch, he added silently. And as long as she worked beside him, humming under her breath and smelling of hay and baby powder. He glanced over at Pete who was doing his best to lure one of the half-wild barn cats into accepting a handful of dried corn.

"I know I should get him a dog," she murmured. They stood side by side and waited for the boy to come down from the loft, where the bushy-tailed gray cat had hidden. Shadows lurked in the corners of the barn where the outside security light couldn't reach. Ellen sighed heavily, and without thinking, Spence draped a companionable arm across her shoulders.

Companionable? Yeah, right.

"They sort of go together. Boys and dogs." In this particular case he sided with Pete.

"He cried for days after Bowser died, but come to think about it, he didn't start asking for another dog until fairly recently."

"That probably means he's healing. Wounds don't last forever, Ellen. That doesn't mean there aren't scars, but after a while even a scar becomes a natural part of—" He shrugged. "You know what I mean."

Did she? Did he? Was he talking about the pain a boy feels when he loses a father or a beloved pet, or the bone-deep grief of a woman who loses a beloved husband?

Something told him he'd better back off. He had enough to handle without diving into those particular waters.

Back in the house, Ellen went through the checklist. "Homework finished?"

"Yes, ma'am."

"Clean clothes laid out for the morning?"

"My green shirt's getting too little, Mom. I'm really growing pretty big, aren't I?"

Spence looked him over with mock severity. "You're going to have to un-grow until your mom can get you some new clothes. Looks to me like those pants are shrinking, too."

From the width of his grin, you'd think the boy had been paid the greatest compliment. Shaking his head, Spence crossed the room and switched off the outside security lights. Given the option, he'd have left them all on—porch lights and barn lights—but Ellen was the one who paid the power bills.

The rest of the nightly ritual involved chocolate milk and cookies. "Can I have seven, Mom? They're real little."

"Three."

"'Kay. Thanks. While I watch TV?"

"Just until the first commercial break."

Tonight's treat was a wildlife special on snakes. Pete, seated cross-legged on the floor, was awed by the anacondas. Spence, seated beside Ellen on the faded slip-covered sofa, murmured that she might want to think about getting him a mutt before he adopted a pet from the wild.

"Go ahead, gang up on me, why don't you?" she teased, and Pete looked around, his avid gaze going from one to the other. The boy was no fool.

After Pete went upstairs, Ellen picked up a book and Spence switched to an all-news channel, eager for any shred of information he could glean that would arm him for the coming confrontation. What he needed was an advance scout to bring him up to speed on what was

going on behind the scenes. Reporters had their
sources, but not all sources were reliable. And all, unfortunately, were subject to bias, deliberate or otherwise.

He could always simply walk into the courtroom unannounced and let the chips fly. If he had only himself
to consider, he might choose to do it that way, but there
were others involved through no fault of their own.
Before he exposed himself, he had to know Ellen and
Pete were safe. If Del Brio knew where he'd been staying these past two weeks, he might put two and two
together and come up with something that made
Spence break out in a cold sweat, just thinking about
it.

A few miles away a hushed meeting was taking
place. Two men stood on a country road. Two cars,
one heavily detailed with a flame motif, were pulled
up under the shelter of a stand of young pine trees.

"Sonofabitch, man, that's no answer! I need answers! I gotta know, damn it! I told Frankie we knew
for sure, that's why he went ahead and got that Joe Ed
Malone guy appointed."

The smaller man hunched his bony shoulders and
looked away. "Shouldn'a told him nothin'."

"It's been two frigging weeks, man! I had to tell
him something. Listen, Sal, the guy's got to be dead.
We checked every place he coulda been holed up and
didn't come up with nothing. You saw that car—nobody could've lived through that. What I want to know
is where the hell's his body?"

"Coulda been sucked out—the door was tore off.
Dogs coulda worked him over, buzzards maybe."

"Then how come his coat didn't get sucked out with him?"

The smaller man shrugged. "Beats me. I'm not the one that give the boss the all clear."

"Hellfire, man, once the cops found his car with all his stuff inside, Frankie was ready to move in. He had Joe Ed Malone all set to take over the minute Harrison was out of the picture."

"Yeah, but we still don't know for sure if he's dead or not. Me, I think he's shacked up wi' that widder woman," Sal said, his voice more of a whine. "These two guys I met in a bar said—"

"I know what they said! You tol' me a hunnert times! You wanna be the one to tell Frankie we was wrong? We don't even know for sure it's the same guy, and I'm tellin' you this, I ain't wearin' no cement boots fer nobody!"

There was more swearing, more frustrated grumbling, then Silent Sal finished using up his month's allotment of words. "Check out the widder's place again, but I ain't doin' him if you find him. Doing a D.A., you're talking big time lethal injection."

"Yeah, well, lemme tell you something, good buddy. If there's a chance this guy Harrison's still alive, one of us better find him fast. If he turns up alive after we told Frankie he was dead, we're gator bait."

The man known as Silent Sal, who wasn't always silent, nodded. Peaches absently scratched his newest tattoo, which showed signs of becoming infected. He knew what he had to do. He'd been doing it ever since he'd knocked over his first convenience store when he was eleven years old, down near the border. He'd shot his first man at the tender age of thirteen, but this was the big league. Screwing up when you were dealing with a man as powerful as Frank Del Brio could give you a bad case of the deads.

Sal stalked off, muttering something under his breath about heading south. Reaching his own nondescript sedan, he turned and pointed at Peaches's pride and joy. "Why'n hell don't you get yourself a car that don't stand out like a dog in a cathouse?"

"Hey, I like art. You got a problem with that?" Peaches slammed the door and started the engine, racing it a couple of times before he backed out. Sal was a pissant. Let him head south. Who needed him? Peaches had a lead through some schoolkid—work 'em right and kids leaked like a gutted muffler. If it checked out and he could produce a dead body—didn't matter how long it'd been dead—old Frankie boy would be choppin' in tall cotton from now on. And the man who'd made it happen would be set for life.

And it wouldn't be Sal.

"Oh, yea-a-ah," the tattooed man crooned softly.

"I warned you about overdoing it," Ellen grumbled. "But no, you had to go and prove something when you're barely off crutches. Here, hold still." Ellen poured a palmful of the smelly liniment and slapped it between his shoulder blades.

"One crutch, not crutch*es*. And it was only for a couple of days to keep you from jawboning me to death." He'd given himself away when it had taken three tries to lever himself up out of the chair.

"Yeah, yeah, yeah. And who had a turnip-size knot on his head?"

"Cantaloupe. It's gone now— Ouch! Don't dig in so hard!"

She pinched him, but they were both grinning. Having her hands on him under any circumstances was good. Incredibly good.

Dangerously good, Spence reminded himself. He forced himself to keep at the front of his mind his dual priorities: bringing down Del Brio's regime and keeping Ellen and Pete safe.

Shifting slightly, he tried to find a comfortable position, but there was none to be found lying facedown on his hard mattress. What he needed was something softer—something that would accommodate the changes that were rapidly taking place in his groin area.

"Thought any more about getting Pete a dog?" He tossed the topic into the ring, desperate for a distraction. Ellen's hands had slowed until the massage was becoming a lot more than just a remedy for sore muscles.

"He won't let me forget. I thought about getting him one for Christmas, but he really needs a new bike. Maybe I can get him a reconditioned bike and a dog from the pound."

Warm, firm palms slid down his spine, then spread out over his hips, where he wasn't sore at all.

"Is that peppermint I smell?" Spence sucked in air through clenched jaws.

"Menthol."

"Yeah. Ah-hh…don't stop. Look, why don't I get him a dog and you can get him the bike?" His voice sounded as if it had been wrung out and hung up to dry.

"You might not be here Christmas," she reminded him, her hands working their way up toward his shoulders, thumbs biting into his flesh.

Spence took one deep breath, then rolled over to stare up at her. She snatched back her hands as if they'd been guilty of some terrible transgression, her attention seemingly focused on the pottery base of the small bedside lamp.

"Ellen, look at me."

"I don't think so," she whispered.

"Damn it, look at me!" When she did, he almost wished he could snatch back the demand. Was that truly sadness he saw in those clear green eyes? For him? That didn't make sense—not that anything had made much sense once he'd gone through lost-and-found and come out on the other side.

But nothing that he knew of involving her had changed in the past few hours. Sitting up, he caught her by the shoulders, shaking her gently. "Ellen, look at me. Hear what I'm telling you. I can stay or I can leave if my being here creates a problem. It's your call. But I want you to know that wherever I am, whatever I'm doing, I will be back. That's a promise."

It was a promise he had no right to make—he didn't even know if she wanted to hear it—but it was a promise he fully intended to keep. For Pete, if that was the way she wanted it, and for himself.

She sighed and offered him a wobbly little smile, but said nothing.

He waited, hardly knowing what it was he was waiting for, hoping for.

Oh, yeah, he knew, all right. Of all the lousy timing.

"Will you?" she whispered.

"You don't believe me?" This was going to be tricky. It could be dangerous for all three of them if he surfaced before he had things set up and someone made the connection between them.

"Storm, it's not that I don't believe you. It's just that—"

It's Spence, damn it—not Storm! But he couldn't tell her that without confessing the whole thing, and right now, the less she knew, the better. She'd denied his presence once. He didn't want her to have to do it again, because this time she might not be able to pull it off. There was a basic honesty about Ellen Wagner that was one of the things he lo—liked so much about her. Del Brio's trained gorillas might not have known she was lying that first night—she hadn't had time to get used to Spence's being here. Next time, if Del Brio sent anyone with an I.Q. larger than his collar size, she'd be a sitting duck.

It was partly frustration, partly spontaneous combustion that made him kiss her. But it was sheer sexual desire that shoved him over the edge, beyond the reach of common sense. He knew—they'd both known right from the first—that no matter how attracted they might be, any deepening of the relationship was asking for trouble.

Well, to hell with playing it safe!

Ten

The pressure had been building for too long. One touch and the kiss caught fire. Groaning against her mouth, he pulled her down on top of him. Awkward at first, she twisted until she was lying half across his body, one of her legs entangled with one of his. The scent of liniment, shampoo and baby power seeped into his senses as her hands moved hungrily over his chest.

He could tell she was as eager as he was. The knowledge added fuel to an already combustible situation. Jake's bed—Jake's jeans—Jake's wife.

But my woman.

She tasted of apples gone winey. If this was all there was, all there could ever be—

He broke off the thought as the taste of her mouth, the feel of her soft warmth drove the last shred of reason from his mind. Somehow, without losing contact with her mouth, he managed to unbutton her shirt. Two fingers found their way inside her bra.

It wasn't enough. He wanted her naked beside him, underneath him, on top of him. Wanted full possession in all the ways a man could possess a woman. "Ellen," he whispered harshly, dragging his mouth from hers. "You know what's happening, don't you?"

Breathing heavily, she nodded.

"If you want to raise an objection, you'd better do it now."

She shook her head, her face still hidden in his throat. "We barely know each other. Only two weeks ago you were a...a stranger," she whispered against the pulse pounding there.

"Oh. Right." Easing a hand down between them, he touched her in a way that made her whimper. "Guess we'd better wait a few more minutes, then."

She stroked his nipples with her menthol-scented fingertips. "I guess we'd better," she mused, though he couldn't tell if she was laughing or panting. They were both breathing audibly.

"I certainly wouldn't want you to think I was rushing you." *Where's your common sense, man? You don't need this kind of trouble!*

It was when her fingers left his nipples and began trailing down his chest, his stomach, to his flat, hard abdomen that he knew there'd be no turning back. The time for reason was past. He could no more deny himself—deny either of them—this moment than the shore could deny the incoming tide.

Desperately, knowing that it would end all too quickly, he tried to store up fragments of time in his mind—fragments involving the sense of taste, of touch and scent. Things were moving too fast. He thought he heard her whisper something like, "Time's up," but his heart was pounding so heavily he couldn't be sure.

Her fingers moved south again. At the first tentative touch, he nearly lost it. Knowing that if she touched him again it would be over before it even began, he snatched her hand up to his mouth and nibbled her fingers, torn between the urge to race toward the finish line and the almost equally powerful need to savor each step along the way.

This was more than foreplay—this touching, tasting

exploration—the rocking, grinding of pelvis against pelvis in sweet anticipation. Playing for time, he whispered, "Peppermint," as his tongue traced the lines across her palm.

"Menthol. It's supposed to relax the muscles."

"Guess again," he whispered, soft laughter erupting that in no way broke the tension. Teasing had never been a part of his sexual repertoire. He'd never particularly missed it, never even thought about it. But then, he'd never before known a woman like Ellen.

"Storm?" she whispered. "We could find out, unless you're afraid."

"Oh, lady, do I look like the kind of man who backs down from a challenge?"

Eyes dancing, she moved her body sinuously against his. He gave up any hope of prolonging the inevitable. With much twisting and squirming, they struggled to shed the rest of their clothes. He had trouble with the gripper at her waist. "Haven't you ever heard of elastic?" he muttered.

"Haven't you ever heard of patience?" she retorted sweetly.

"Patience and short fuses don't go together." Truer words, he told himself, shuddering, had never been spoken. He brought her hands to his lips again and kissed each finger, then placed them on his body, giving her silent permission to resume explorations.

And resume, she did. "You're so hard...everywhere," she marveled. Talking was something else that had never played much part in his sex life. "Like one of those TV advertisements for exercise equipment."

As if she knew how it affected him—Judas priest, she had to know! It wasn't something a man could hide—she took great joy in slowly dragging her hands down his torso, across his abdomen, circling his navel. Reaching his groin, she traced the crease of his thighs, her fingertips brushing against the thicket of dark hair.

He groaned. "You're killing me by degrees."

"I was trying to go slow, in case the liniment burns," she murmured as her hands closed around his rigid shaft.

"If I get any hotter," he said through clenched teeth, "we're going to be setting off your smoke detectors. Ellen—" Hanging onto control by a thread, he covered her hands with his own. "This isn't going to work."

"It said right there on the tube that it was great for relaxing stiffness, but you're right—it's not working. D'you think I should ask for my money back?"

His short burst of laughter turned into a groan, and then both of them passed beyond the point of words.

Abruptly reversing their position, Spence knelt over her, parting her thighs with hands that were far from steady. In the dim glow of the bedside lamp, he studied her openly, first reverently touching her breasts, cupping them, stroking the hardened tips. By then, all thought of teasing was past; the only reality was this throbbing obsession, this urgent demand for completion.

Wait! Make it last! He lowered himself carefully until he was just touching her, forcing himself to hold back until she was ready.

Clasping him by the waist, she tried to bring him inside her. "Now, now, please!"

Yes! Thrusting slowly, withdrawing, thrusting again, he managed to hold back another split second as the pulsating tension built to explosive dimensions. She moaned, her short nails biting convulsively into his buttocks. Slowly, he thrust again and this time his control snapped. Mentholated heat eddied around them, mingled with the intoxicating scent of sex as she lifted her hips and eagerly met each thrust. The exquisite, pulsating pleasure increased, tightening around them, binding them together, as clinging, gripping, panting, they rode out the storm together, stroke by powerful stroke.

Both bodies bathed in sweat, she convulsed around him, triggering his own release. Dimly he was aware of the sound of the soft cascading cries that fell like a benediction around them as they collapsed in a tangle of damp, throbbing flesh.

Not until much later did it occur to Spence that he hadn't used protection. He hoped she was taking something, but it was his responsibility. I'll be here, he vowed silently. Whatever it takes, I'll be here for you.

Ellen was gone when he awoke. Dressing hastily despite soreness in a few muscles that hadn't been sore yesterday, Spence hurried out to the barn. He had to see her—had to know that she was all right with what had happened. Needed to tell her the full truth, especially now.

"I think Moxie's going into labor," she announced, meeting him halfway between barn and house. "I'm going inside to call the vet to see if there's anything in particular I need to watch for."

"It's a pretty natural process. Wild horses have been doing it for thousands of years."

She shot him a dirty look. "My husband didn't spend his last penny to buy a bunch of wild horses. If anything happens to Moxie, it's more than an investment, it's Pete's future."

Message received. Last night was not to be mentioned. From now until that horse dropped her foal, whatever he had to tell her—whatever was between the two of them—was on hold.

Fine. He could live with that. "Go call, I'll baby-sit the mare. Where's Pete?"

"He's in with her. I know he should be in school, but for today, I think this is more important."

"Biology lesson."

"Whatever," she said, not meeting his eyes as she strode past him.

Damn it, he should never have taken her to bed. As if things weren't complicated enough, now he couldn't look at her without remembering—without wanting her again. Just how long, he wondered, did it take for a man to get so screwed up there was no way back? When had his priorities undergone a shift that would've registered on any seismograph?

Pete was seated in a pile of clean straw just outside the mare's stall. The other horses had been led outside. "Know what? Moxie's gonna have her baby. Mom said I could stay and help, but don't go in there, 'cause she's nervous. See, she's never done it before and she might forget I'm her friend and kick me."

Gingerly, Spence lowered himself to sit beside the boy. "Looks like you've pretty much got everything under control," he observed. The mare was moving around, but didn't seem overly agitated.

For several minutes neither of them spoke. Then Pete said, "Did I tell you Mr. Ludlum used to play baseball? Did you ever play baseball?" And then he caught himself and added, "Oh, yeah. I forgot your am-a-nesia."

Spence didn't bother to correct him. Telling Ellen was going to be tough enough. Telling Pete that he had another life, a demanding career that required his presence now more than ever, was going to be even tougher.

"I could show you how to pitch a curve ball if you want," Pete offered. "I'm pretty good."

"You got a deal, but let's wait until after Moxie does her thing, okay? Your mama might need us."

"Yeah, she pro'ly does. I help her a lot, but it's not like when Mr. Caster was here. Or my dad."

No, it wasn't like that, Spence told himself. It would never be like that. He was a district attorney in the middle of the fight of his life—possible even for his life. And while there was something increasingly seductive about Ellen's small ranch, about the woman herself, about the boy, about the hard, satisfying work and the easygoing camaraderie—not to mention what had happened last night—he had places to go. People to see. And no idea of how long it would all take.

The two men met on the course at the Lone Star Country Club near the ninth hole tee. Flynt Carson lifted his club, took a few practice swings, then lowered it again. "What've you found out?"

"About which, Spence or Luke?"

"Both. Either."

Tyler scratched his nose. "Luke's situation is out of our hands pending further intelligence. The military's in on it now. They'll get word out as soon as they get a lead. As for Spence, have you considered the possibility of an alien abduction? Damn it, I've combed every square inch of interstate between his apartment and the state pen, fanning out several miles on both sides. We're starting now on the secondary roads. There's a lot of open farm country between Laredo and

Corpus, but I have to tell you, it doesn't look good. If he's alive we'd have heard from him.''

Removing his sunglasses, Flynt wiped the lenses on the sleeve of his knit shirt. "Maybe. Maybe not. If he had a reason to drop out of sight…''

"And let Del Brio move Joe Ed Malone into his slot? I don't think so.''

"You got any better ideas?''

"I'm thinking, I'm thinking. Look, it's a straight shot on the interstate, but we know now from his credit card records that he took the long route. Why?''

Flynt shrugged. "You know Spence. He always claimed he did some of his clearest thinking while he was driving. Reflexes on automatic, mind clear to work on whatever's on the agenda.''

"Yeah, well, we both know he was hoping to get Black to turn state's evidence,'' Tyler said. "Trouble is, he never made it that far. I've got a nasty feeling his health might be endangered if we don't find him fast. I had to barter my soul to keep that reporter from making a major deal out of his disappearance—told him something big was about to bust wide open and promised him an exclusive.''

"Him and how many others?''

"Four…maybe it was five. Look, we both know Del Brio's had his men out beating the bushes. If they find him first…''

Flynt shook his head slowly. "He wouldn't stand a chance now that the switch has been made. We can tell the attorney general that Joe Ed Malone is crooked as a snake, but without solid evidence, his hands are tied.''

"For all we know, the attorney general's been bought and paid for, too.''

Flynt looked up sharply. "You know something I don't?"

"He's clean as far as I know, but that's just it. There's too much we don't know."

"We do know this much, though—without evidence, we're nowhere."

Tyler squinted against the low angle of the December sun. "What we need is incontrovertible proof. And if anyone can come up with that, it's Spence. I'm pretty sure he had almost enough when he disappeared. I suspect his office was gone over with a fine-tooth comb, computers and all, but whether or not anything was found, we don't know."

"Which takes us back to the starting line. Where the hell is he? I've checked every morgue and hospital between Laredo, Corpus and Brownsville. We can't go to the local police without knowing for sure who's been turned and who hasn't."

"What gets me is why any man would walk away and leave his papers—hell, his credit cards—in plain sight. My contact says they were found intact by one of Frankie's goons, but the car was totaled. It's almost like he disappeared deliberately. If Del Brio had gotten to him, a body would have turned up by now."

"Which means our guy figured that by dropping out of the picture, he could buy enough time to put together enough proof to blow this mess out of the water once and for all. When that twister came along—"

"It was too good an opportunity to miss," Tyler finished for him.

"You got it. It would be a smart move."

"And our man Spence has never been called stupid."

* * *

Spence Harrison frowned over the glue job on a broken model airplane. He'd set out a plate of cheese, pickle slices, salsa and sandwich meat, made a fresh pot of coffee, and then he'd waited. Now that he'd made up his mind to tell her, he wanted to get it off his chest. When he made his next move, it would have to be fast. There might not be time at that point for explanations.

Ellen kicked off her boots and came inside in a breath of cool, fresh air. "It won't be long now," she said. "Oh, good, food! I'm starved!"

"How's Pete holding out?"

"In hog heaven."

"In what?"

"Didn't I happen to mention I'm only half Texan? My mama was the daughter of a North Carolina hog baron. Every now and then she would slip up and let her roots show. It used to drive Daddy wild."

"Your father married the daughter of a hog farmer and then broke off with you for marrying a soldier?"

"Don't turn up your nose at hog farmers, not unless you're willing to give up bacon, ham and pork chops." She poked her head into the refrigerator and came up with a jar of mayonnaise. "Anyway, I like to think I got my business sense from Daddy and my common sense from Mama. At least I think she had some, but to tell the truth, I hardly remember her. You can see for yourself how far the Summerlin business savvy has taken me."

He chuckled. Couldn't help it. When she was running on fumes, she didn't bother to maintain her defensive walls. "Oh, I don't know. Seems to me you're about to increase your assets by a healthy percentage."

"I've already increased my vet bills by an even healthier percentage." She added another layer to her creation and topped it off with a dash of black pepper. "Pete's decided now that he wants to be a veterinarian." She eyed him, obviously waiting for a reaction.

"And you're not happy with the decision, right? Ellen, the kid's only eight years old. He's still got a few more stages to go through before he settles on a career. Fireman, jet pilot, rodeo rider."

"Don't forget baseball player." Lowering her gaze, she concentrated on trimming the ragged edges off her sandwich. "I'd sort of planned on our breeding horses, you know? Maybe even training them."

"That was Jake's dream. Why not let your son figure out his own? Chances are, he'll come around, given time."

She took a big bite and chewed, silent for so long he had to wonder if he'd overstepped some invisible boundary. The walls had definitely been there earlier, but he'd thought they were down again.

"Tell me something, Storm, did you follow in your father's footsteps? Oops…sorry, forget I asked." Yeah, she was edgy, all right. He had a feeling it wasn't entirely about the mare, either. Was she thinking the same thing he was? About how good last night had been…and how soon they could manage an encore?

Which was unlikely, at least for the foreseeable future.

"I know I certainly didn't follow my father's dream," she went on in that same brittle tone. "His dream was to triple his inheritance, expand his investment business and produce a slew of sons to carry on the Summerlin name. Instead he produced a single daughter who stubbornly refused to marry his gold-plated candidate."

"Thank God for that," Spence muttered. "At least you gave him a grandson."

"No, I didn't. My father's never even met Pete. He wouldn't help me when I desperately needed help—I actually begged. Well, now that I don't need his help, it'll be a cold day in hell before I let him get his hands on my son."

She didn't need her father's help? To Spence's way of thinking, she was about as needy as a woman could be. If not to her father, then where could she turn for help? To another husband?

The thought was distinctly unwelcome. Leaning back in his chair, he found he could easily picture her against a different background. Surprising, as he'd never seen her wearing anything but those baggy work clothes or a tattered chenille bathrobe.

Ellen took another bite of her sandwich, chewed thoughtfully, swallowed and took a sip of coffee. "Okay, so if Pete wants to be a vet, that's still connected to horses. I'll simply find a way to send him to school. There's plenty of time to save up."

"To save up what?" It was cruel to remind her that she barely even had an income, but there were times when a man had to be cruel to be kind. Someone had to force her to look reality squarely in the face.

She shrugged. "The horses won't always be a drain. I can probably count on two more foals about every two or three years. If most of them turn out to be mares, when they grow up to breeding age..."

"There you go," Spence said softly, because he didn't know what else to say. Or rather, he knew, but she wouldn't want to hear it. They were both well aware of all that could go wrong in the meantime.

"Things will work out, you'll see," she said with a

lift of that stubborn, vulnerable chin that made him want to gather her in his arms and shelter her from reality.

Sure they would. "They have a way of doing that, you know," he said. Except when they didn't.

She looked at him then—really looked at him. "Something's happened, hasn't it? I mean besides…you know. Last night."

"What makes you say that?"

She shrugged. "I don't know, woman's intuition again?"

"Yeah, something's happened, Ellen."

Eleven

Spence knew he couldn't put it off any longer. Things had been on hold far too long. Direct by nature, he was sick of having to skirt around the truth. Now that he finally knew the truth—or at least the part that showed above the horizon—he had to level with her.

Ellen never once interrupted. Once or twice she looked as if she wanted to, but he didn't give her an opening. Quickly, unemotionally, he told her who he was and where he'd been going when he'd been side-lined, adding the fact that he was unmarried and was not now, nor had he been in recent years, seriously involved with a woman. He didn't imagine the look of relief that flashed across her face.

"So there you have it," he said when he was finished. "We both came pretty close to guessing the truth."

"My God," she whispered in an awed tone when he finished the bare-bones summary. "Why wasn't there more in the paper about your disappearance? I remember just one small story—oh, and wasn't there another piece about whatshisname being appointed in your place? I should think the disappearance of an important court official would warrant headlines in all the major Texas papers. Maybe it did. I only know what was in the *Clarion*. But what I read made it sound like you were taking an extended vacation or something."

"Granted, it was played down, but then, Lone Star County's not exactly the center of the universe. They have to make editorial decisions, and they went with the really important events, like the high school football scores and the church bazaar's cake sale."

"Stop it, this is serious."

"Yeah, I know." Hell, it bothered him, too. "Okay, I'm guessing someone covered for me."

"But how, why?"

"Ellen, there's something I didn't tell you. I'm not at liberty to divulge all the details, but when I tangled with that twister I was on my way to prison to take an important deposition." One he'd hoped would point him in the direction of some pretty telling evidence, if he'd been lucky. And careful. "As things stand now, the fewer people who know I'm still alive, the better. Which means I'd appreciate it if you didn't tell anyone."

"I won't, of course. Not even Pete?"

He hesitated for a long time. "Look, Ellen, I don't want to simply disappear, and I definitely don't want to have to lie to Pete any more than I already have, but you have to understand…these people I'm trying to bring down wouldn't hesitate to use you or Pete to get to me."

Carefully she laid half a sandwich on her plate. Her face was a few degrees paler, her eyes darker, larger. "What do you mean, 'use' us?"

"Just what you think I mean. If they had any reason to believe you were important to me, they'd know that by threatening you and Pete, they'd gain complete control over me."

After a long silence she whispered, "But only if you cared."

"Any decent man—" He sighed. He couldn't lie to her, not again. Yet how could he tell her how much he was coming to care when he was trying his damnedest not to care? He wasn't ready. Not now, maybe not ever, depending on how things worked out. She didn't need any more losses.

"Ellen, about last night…"

Reaching across the table, she covered his hand with hers. "Don't. It should never have happened, but it did, and I'm not sorry."

"I promised you I'd be there for you if…you know. I mean, we didn't use protection last night."

"Don't even think about that now. You've got enough on your mind. Are you leaving right away? You can take one of the trucks. Take the small one. You can leave it somewhere for me to collect later. The tank's full, and if I have to go into town, I can drive the duelly. Do you need to call someone first?"

"I had a cell phone with me when all hell broke loose." He smiled, but it faded quickly. "I also had a brand-new car, the top half of a good suit, a tape recorder, a briefcase and a few other things I've probably forgotten about." He would worry about the car later. With any luck it hadn't fallen in the wrong hands. "Right now what I need is to figure out some way to get in touch with a couple of friends without broadcasting my present whereabouts."

"A phone call?"

"Not from your number. I honestly don't think anything would come of it, but those two guys who came around the night of the storm had to have had some reason to check this place out. I don't know where my car was found, or if it ever was, but the more I think about it, the more I wonder if they didn't have a tail on me as soon as I left town that day. A few more miles out of town and I might have had a fatal accident. The weather just fouled up their plans.''

"Oh, God. If anyone had had to get caught in that twister, why couldn't it have been those two creeps?''

"I'm not sure they'd have both fit into your wheelbarrow.''

She ignored his feeble attempt at a joke. "At least I didn't tell them anything.''

"How about your friends, Booker and Clyde? They know exactly how long I've been here. For that matter, Pete might have mentioned something to his friend Joey. No reason why he wouldn't...we didn't ask him not to.''

She lowered her face to her hands. "Oh, Lord. It never even occurred to me.''

"Of course it didn't. Look, this is probably just a mild case of paranoia on my part, but humor me, will you? Another couple of days won't matter after this length of time. It'll give me a chance to think of some way to make contact with certain people and to find out what's going on behind the scenes before I make my grand comeback.'' Meanwhile he could work out some way to protect her until he had things under control again.

"Then you'll stay here?''

It was the hope he saw glowing in those clear green eyes that nearly broke him. "Another day or so, if that's all right. By tomorrow or the next day I should have a pretty good idea of how things are shaping up in town. Once I do, I can figure out the best way to deal with it.''

Neither of them spoke for several moments. Spence wasn't thinking about the situation in Mission Creek, he was thinking instead about what was going to happen in the downstairs bedroom once Pete had gone upstairs and they were sure he'd fallen asleep. God knows, he had no business involving her any more than she already was, but it was too late now. That particular genie was already out of the bottle.

"Ellen—"

They could hear Pete yelling all the way from the barn. "Mama, Mama, come quick!"

Ellen jumped up from the table. So did Spence. They raced out to the barn expecting the worst and found, instead, a wet, shaky foal, barely out of the sac.

Pete scampered back up the side of the stall, hanging over the slatted sides. "Look at it, Mom. See? Moxie did it all by herself! She didn't cry or anything, either, and boy, I bet it hurt real bad!"

The rest of the day, naturally enough, was taken up with admiring the new foal and checking on Miss Sara, who seemed more irritable than usual. Pete said it was because she was jealous. Moxie had a baby and Miss Sara didn't.

"I expect you're right. We'll keep a close watch on her," Spence told him.

The vet showed up a few hours later and pronounced the new arrival sound. Pete said, "Can we call him Bowser?"

So much for adding to her breeding stock, Ellen thought ruefully. "Bowser's a fine name, but wouldn't you rather save it for when you get a new dog?"

Pete tilted his head thoughtfully. "It wouldn't be right to have two dogs named Bowser, but this Bowser's a horse, so that's okay."

While he was there Doc Leonard checked on Miss Sara and predicted that she'd drop her own foal within the next twenty-four hours. "Cross your fingers that this one's a girl," Ellen said, hiding her disappointment over the new male addition to her breeding herd. Maybe she'd have done better breeding rabbits, only there wasn't much of a market for them.

Just before dark, claiming long-neglected bookkeeping, Ellen suggested Spence and Pete go exercise the geldings while she brought her records up to date. "If we're going to establish a creditable breeding operation here, I've got to record every detail."

"You mean like who the mama is and who the daddy is," Pete said.

"Even the grandparents. I've got all the papers, I just haven't looked at them in ages. You two run along, have a nice ride, and I'll get caught up here before Miss Sara goes into action."

They rode out to the work site. They'd made a good start on repairing the fence before dark last night, but there was still work to be done. Spence said, "What do you say we finish up today? One of us can wait here and the other one can go get the truck and bring the tools."

"I'll go get the truck," Pete said, two big front teeth flashing in his thin, tanned face.

"Yeah, you do that. Your mama needs something else to worry about."

"We could both go and I could steer while you did the other stuff. Mr. Caster let me steer the John Deere once, and he said I was a natural."

"How about we get the fencing done and then worry about driving lessons?"

"Cool!"

Spence knew he'd spoken too hastily the minute the

words left his mouth. A plan was beginning to come together in his mind as he stood, feet apart, hands on his hips, and looked down the row of wire fencing that had been erected back when the land had held cattle instead of grapefruit trees.

Pete, planting his small booted feet apart and his hands on his hips in an unconscious imitation, nodded soberly. "Yeah, we'd better finish the fence first, then we can teach me to drive."

The work went better than expected. They finished up well before dark, and then Spence ran the bench seat back as far as it would go and let Pete sit on the edge in front of him and steer. The ruts mostly did the job for him, but by the time they pulled up beside the tractor shed, the kid was grinning from ear to ear. In hog heaven, as Ellen would have said.

"Can I practice shifting gears tomorrow?"

"Let's not rush it. Give the first lesson time to sink in."

"Yeah," Pete said softly, his big dark eyes glowing in anticipation.

Spence could have kicked himself. Things were bad enough without setting up any false expectations.

Ellen protested that she really should set up a cot in the barn, but there was never any real question of who was going to sleep where. Or with whom. She said if he was still sore, a hot bath in the tub upstairs might help. There was only the small shower downstairs they'd had installed when the pantry and utility room had been combined to make another bedroom.

A cold shower might have made more sense under the circumstances, but they both knew what was going to happen. And wise or not, he wasn't going to turn away. So while Spence soaked some of the soreness from muscles unaccustomed to such physical activity, Ellen made one last check on the mares. By the time he pulled the plug on what had to be the fastest tub bath in recorded history, he barely had the patience to dry off. While he was shaving off his late-day growth of beard—that much, at least, he could do for her—he heard the downstairs shower running.

Bath towel knotted around his hips, he hurried down the stairs. Ellen was already there, in his bed. The small bedside lamp shone warmly on her tangle of damp, dark hair and he remembered that her hair dryer, along with all her other gear, was still upstairs.

Not that it mattered. She was beautiful just as she was, lying in his bed with the spread pulled up to her shoulders. No false modesty, no pretense that she didn't know what was about to happen. That was one of the things he liked most about her—her honesty. In his line of work, all the players worked an angle.

Not Ellen. As some sage had once remarked, "What you see is what you get," and God knew he wanted what he saw. Wanted it so much he was shivering.

"I found some, um— They're in the drawer."

It had been twenty-one years since Spence had had his first woman. She'd been nineteen, five years older than he was at the time. He hadn't been nearly as nervous then as he was now.

"Yeah…that is, thanks. I mean—"

"Spence."

"Huh?"

"Come to bed."

Shaking his head, he had to grin. To think he'd once considered himself pretty sophisticated, a suave man-about-town.

After that there were few words. It was as if both of them knew that this might be the last time they would be together this way. He dropped his towel and she gazed openly at his naked body, as if to memorize it. Reaching up, she placed her hands on his sides and began to stroke, pulling him down beside her. "I love the way you look, all sleek and firm and muscular. The way you feel."

The way he felt was explosive. Combustible. Spence stood it for as long as he could before he joined her on the bed. Leaning over, he braced his weight on his hands, determined to make it last as long as possible. Not until the instant before his lips touched hers did he close his eyes. Rocking his mouth against the moist softness of hers, he angled his face, tugging her lips apart.

Take it easy. Make it last. There might not be a second chance.

Taking it easy was never an option. Taking advantage of that one small opening, he deepened the kiss, abandoning any pretense of a more leisurely approach in the face of his increasingly desperate hunger. Her skin was warm and soft and smelled of soap, baby powder and essence of Ellen. If he lived to be a hundred years old, he would never forget it—never forget this sweet, independent, sexy, wonderful woman with the callused hands and the incendiary touch.

Conscious of the fleeting moments, he took the time to pay homage to each part of her body. Her breasts with the dark, rigid peaks and the shallow valley between them, her narrow waist, the gentle flare of her hips and the soft cradle of her belly.

When the dark thicket between her thighs drew his gaze, his touch, and eventually, his lips, she shuddered

convulsively. He savored her there, then groaned and
rose quickly above her. In the warm glow of lamplight,
he found her ineffably beautiful and told her so, his
voice gruff with emotion, and when she closed her
eyes, her lashes were gleaming with moisture.

This won't be the last time, he vowed silently. He
had no right to make promises—had no way of knowing where he would be tomorrow or if he'd even be
alive. If tonight was all they could share, he would do
his best to make it a memorable one.

Turning aside, he opened the drawer in the bedside
table with one hand. A moment later, when he moved
over her, she was ready, lips parted, eyes glowing
softly. He could see the faint flutter of her heart echoed
in the shadows of her breasts.

Carefully, he positioned himself and slowly entered
her. This time there was a sense of inevitability in the
act, almost a sense of sadness.

One thrust, and then like spark to tinder, they burst
into flames. She wrapped her long, cool legs around
his waist and whimpered, her fingers clutching his
sweat-damp sides as together they raced toward the ex-
plosion of sheer, unimaginable pleasure.

Long after the race ended, she lay in his arms,
breathing softly through parted lips. "I need to…" she
began drowsily, and he laid a finger over her mouth,
still swollen from his kisses.

"Shh, you need to stay here until I decide whether
or not I'll need that crutch again to get out of bed."

She smiled. At least he thought she did. Moving his
head to look was too great an effort at the moment.

"Stay here. There's no need for you to get up, but
I really should go out to check on things in the barn
again."

"You stay here. I'll go check on the girls," Spence said without opening his eyes.

Neither of them made a move to get up. Spence wasn't at all sure he could walk. Aftershocks still reverberated through his body from what had to have been the most profound sexual experience of his entire life. He didn't know if the aura of danger had added the extra element, or if it was sensing that this might be the last time.

"Knowing Pete," Ellen said, "he's probably sneaked downstairs and is camping out in the barn."

"Let's hope Miss Sara waits awhile before going into her act. I don't think I want him bursting in here right now with a progress report."

"I'd better get up," Ellen said sleepily.

"I'll go. If Pete's in the barn, do you want him to come inside?"

"Wouldn't do any good. He'd just hang out his bedroom window trying to see what was going on."

"Mmm..." He nuzzled the place behind her ear where she was incredibly sensitive. He had discovered more than one place on her body where a single kiss could have her gasping for breath.

But as it turned out, they both got up. Just as Spence was reaching for the bedside table drawer again, the phone rang in the kitchen. He froze. Ellen sat up, grabbed her bathrobe and went to answer it. Who the devil would be calling at this time of night? Spence wondered as he pulled on a pair of jeans. The vet? Hardly. The old guy had struck him as adequate, but about ten years past retirement age. Besides, why would old Doc Leonard be calling at this hour?

"Hello?" Ellen said hesitantly. He could hear her

clearly through the door she'd left open. After a brief pause she said, "Who's calling? Who is this?"

Zipping his fly, Spence hurried into the kitchen to see her standing there, the phone dangling from its cord. The look on her face was more puzzled than frightened.

Catching sight of him, she said, "That was odd. It was for you...I think." From the other side of the room, Spence could hear the dial tone. She made no move to hang up the receiver.

"Ellen?"

"He said— It was this man. When I said 'Hello?' he said, 'Tell your sweetheart we'll be paying him a visit.'"

The room was not particularly cold, but Spence felt as if he'd just been doused with a bucket of ice water. "And when you asked who was calling?"

"He just said, 'You tell him that, you hear?'"

Twelve

Ellen finished putting on her bathrobe and made coffee, then raced upstairs to check on Pete, who was sound asleep in his own bed. Evidently the fencing plus the preliminary driving lesson had worn him out.

They agreed that the horses would have to wait. Whatever was going on was serious, possibly even dangerous. Even now Ellen shuddered, remembering the sound of that gravely voice on the phone.

Wordlessly, she placed a cup of black coffee on the table at Spence's elbow. Funny, she thought, how quickly she'd gotten used to thinking of him as Spence and not Storm. Although he'd apparently been in the middle of a storm that had nothing to do with the weather when she'd found him.

Finders keepers. The childish phrase popped into her mind, and she shoved it away. She was just beginning to realize that no matter how intimately she knew this man, he wasn't hers to keep. Up until two weeks ago he'd had a full life that hadn't included her at all.

He was talking now to someone named Flynt. "I have a feeling time's running out, so let's make this fast and get off the line. Here's what I need." Speaking rapidly, he proceeded to read off the items he'd scribbled on the back of her grocery list.

The man sprawled out on one of her kitchen chairs, barefoot, bare-chested, the top of his jeans undone, was a stranger, Ellen told herself. A stranger who snapped out questions and demands as if he were used to being in command.

"Someplace that can't be connected—something well off the beaten track."

Was he describing her farm? Connected to what? To whom? It was most definitely off the beaten track.

By the time he finished she was too furious to listen to the rest of the conversation, which was cryptic, at best. The moment he hung up, she nailed him to the wall with a furious glare. "What do you mean, you're going to need a place to stash a woman and an eight-year old boy?" she snapped.

"Shhh, don't wake Pete. Calm down and I'll explain."

"Nobody stashes me and my son anywhere. Besides, my horses are right in the middle of having their babies. I can't walk out now."

If his nerves weren't on razor edge, Spence might have been amused by the small bundle of fury glaring at him as if he were a mouse she'd just discovered in her lingerie drawer. "Back off, Ellen. Things are coming together faster than I'd expected. Unfortunately, you and Pete are involved." He broke off, paced a tight circle, massaging the back of his neck with one hand, his mind racing down half a dozen avenues at once. "All right, the first thing we have to do is get you and Pete somewhere where you'll be out of the line of fire if worse comes to worst."

"What do you mean, the line of fire? Shooting? You mean—"

"I'm trying to tell you what I mean," he explained with patience dredged up from some deep reservoir. "The men who came looking for me were part of the mob. The Texas Mafia.'' She gasped. He waited to let it sink in. ''Honey, I told you they played hardball. The case I was working on when I got sidetracked involved the murder of a federal judge—a man who's responsible for my being who I am and what I am today, instead of just one more bad apple. The guy who's on trial for Judge Bridges's murder is named Alex Black.''

''I remember reading something awhile back...''

Spence nodded. Quickly he outlined the case in which he hoped to discover who was pulling the defendant's strings. Black might have done the hit, but professional hit men didn't kill for the fun of it, they killed for the money. Spence needed to know who had paid him and why. And whether or not it had anything to do with the fact that it had been Carl Bridges who had cleared Spence and his two closest friends of any implication in the disappearance of Haley Mercado, a woman who had supposedly drowned.

But that was another story, and right now time was at a premium. When he'd been knocked off course by that twister, he had already gathered most of the evidence needed to put a crimp in the mob's activities for the next ten to twenty years. On the verge of documenting the last piece of the puzzle to turn it over to the FBI, fate in the form of the weather had intervened.

Ellen opened her mouth to ask a question—he had offered her only the sketchiest of explanations. He couldn't afford to tell her any more, even if he'd had the time.

''Now listen, I want you to call your father and—''

''My father? No way. Absolutely not!'' She plopped down onto the chair across the table, then jumped up again.

His patience already badly frayed, Spence tried again. "Ellen, I'm not asking you to go hat in hand, begging for favors. You said before that you'd never do that, and I can appreciate your feelings, but for Pete's sake— What I mean is—" He broke off and swore. "Oh, hell, just listen to me, all right? Now, you mentioned your father's bodyguard."

"Driver."

"You said bodyguard."

"I exaggerated. Howard was hired as a driver, but he was an ex-policeman, so he sort of doubled as a bodyguard."

"All right, all right. The thing is, if your father's the kind of man I think he is, you'll be safe there. At least as safe as anywhere I can come up with on short notice. Even safe houses take some arranging, and under the circumstances we can't even be sure their security hasn't been compromised."

She was scared. She was trembling. She was also as stubborn as one of those locust fence posts he'd worn himself out wrestling into submission.

"Ellen, time's passing and we've got to come up with something. The sooner we get started, the better. My friend will locate a place, but it might not be what you're used to. You'd be a whole lot better off with your father."

"I told you—"

They were both on their feet by now. Spence, with a feeling of trouble closing in on him, practically shouted, "Damn it, I can't just walk off and leave you and Pete here alone!"

"We were alone before I dug you out of that ditch. We'll be alone once you're gone." Her chin trembled when she spoke, and he forced himself to calm down.

One thing he'd always been known for, even back in the days of his wild and reckless youth, was coolness under fire.

"All right, then, we'll just have to come up with something else. In a few minutes I should have some answers. Either you can go along with whatever arrangements have been made on your behalf or I roll you up in a rug, toss you into the back of the truck and haul you to—" He'd been about to say his apartment, but that would be the last place to stash her. The first place anyone would look. His ranch was out of the question for the same reason. "To the freight office and ship you off to your father C.O.D," he finished, dangerously close to losing it again.

Before she could return fire, the battle was interrupted by the arrival of reinforcements. Greatly relieved, Spence crossed to the windows, twitched aside the hopsack curtains and peered outside. Two dark SUVs pulled up into the shadow of the tractor shed. Ellen hurried to switch on the outside lights, her eyes round as saucers. "I have a shotgun," she whispered.

"Thanks, honey, but these are our guys. You can stand down now."

She looked at him as if she thought he'd lost his mind. All things considered, it wasn't outside the realm of possibility, he admitted with a wry touch of irony.

Ellen went to brush past him and, acting on impulse, he caught her in his arms and kissed her soundly before she could utter a single protest. "There," he said, reeling slightly from the effect. Or maybe the effects of the past two weeks—the past few hours, in particular. "That'll have to last us for the duration."

It was Spence who opened the door for the new arrivals. "If you guys ever want a career change, I'd recommend Nascar."

"I distinctly heard you say you were running out of time."

"You heard right. Look, there's a lot to explain, but first I need to know…" And then he saw the men staring at Ellen.

Well, hell, what man wouldn't? He made the introductions quickly. "Ellen, this is Flynt Carson." Spence indicated the tall, sandy-haired man with the unsmiling face. "And this is Tyler Murdoch. They're both old friends. You can trust them with your life." Unfortunately, it might come down to just that. "Guys, this is Ellen Wagner. Her son, Pete, is sleeping upstairs. Other than that, the place is empty."

Tyler, dark and ruggedly handsome, nodded and said, "Ma'am." To Spence he said, "I recruited Jose and Donita. They're up for it, they know horses and besides, they owe me a favor. Nita's out there now looking over the stock while Jose checks out the perimeter."

Flynt glanced through the drawn draperies. "We'd better get a move on, folks. It's starting to get light."

"Much traffic?" Spence wasn't too concerned about a tail, as the whole thing had been set up so hurriedly. But then, he hadn't stayed alive for thirty-five years by taking things for granted.

"All clear. Be good if we can get out of here within the next twenty minutes, though."

Ellen looked from one speaker to the other, a dazed expression on her pale face. Spence couldn't much blame her. She hadn't asked for any of this, yet she'd been tossed into deep, shark-filled waters with no warning. This was the only life boat he had to offer and from the way she was looking at him, she didn't quite trust it not to sink with all hands on board.

"You sound like…like some kind of agents. Tell me you don't smear black paint on your faces and jump out of airplanes."

"Nothing so glamorous, I'm afraid." It was Spence who answered. "I'll fill you in on their résumés when we have more time. Things are moving a little too fast right now. I want to get you and Pete away from here before we have any unexpected visitors."

"Spence, I told you—"

"It's just for the duration."

"I am not—underline that—*not* going home to my father. When and if I do, it won't be when I need something from him."

Flynt looked at Ellen, then looked at Tyler and shrugged. Spence had no trouble interpreting the look. *Our friend here is in more trouble than he let on.*

"Okay, message received," he said to Ellen. "When and if you go back home, it'll be on your own terms. Look, we've burnt up too much time arguing already, so you're just going to have to accept whatever arrangements have been made. Do we have a deal?"

Pride was something he could understand and even admire, but this was a hell of a time to have to skirt around a family feud. He turned to Tyler Murdoch. "What have you got lined up?"

"Ever hear of Greasy Pond? It's about ten miles east of town. No connection to any of us. Couple dozen fishing shacks. Old geezer who runs the place minds his own business. I did him a favor a few months ago. He says most of the shacks are empty now, so I put a hold on three together. I can have security moved in before we get there, if Ms. Wagner doesn't mind roughing it for a few days.''

"Ellen?"

"Fine! Whatever! If I have to go, I'll go. But I'm on record as not liking it, y'hear?''

"Protest duly noted,'' Spence said.

"What about my horses? What about my house?''

"The couple they brought in will take care of everything. You won't be gone long. Give me a couple of days to set certain wheels in motion, and you'll be back home before you know it.''

Ellen's face was pale, her eyes wide and wary. Spence knew what she was thinking, but damn it, there was no time for reassurances. Not the kind he wanted to make at any rate. And definitely not with an audience.

"We'd better start moving, then.'' It was the dark, rugged-looking Tyler who spoke, after signaling someone through the window. "Jose and Donita will look after things here, don't worry about that. They're both special agents, but they know horses.''

"What kind of agents? They don't know my horses.''

Any other woman and Spence swore silently he'd have dumped her into a trunk, hauled her out and stashed her in the SUV for her own good. He was tempted, damned if he wasn't. "Honey, let's face it— neither do you. You've got some book learning, but not a whole lot of practical experience. Jose was born on a ranch. When he's not on a mission for— Well, never mind that. Suffice it to say he's spent years working with horses in one capacity or another. Donita barrel-raced her way to a state championship, so your stock will be in excellent hands. Besides, it'll all be over in a few days.'' I sincerely hope, he added silently.

"This place you're taking us…this Greasy Pond place? What will we do there? Where will you be? How will we know when it's safe to come home?"

Gently, Spence placed a finger over her lips. "Don't worry about that right now, worry about how much you want to tell Pete while you're packing enough to last for a few days. You've got five minutes. Go!"

Ellen raked her hands through her hair, leaving it standing on end. With one bleak look, she went. Spence knew he hadn't heard the last of it, not by a long shot. He was going to have a whale of a lot of explaining to do when this business was all over, but for now, at least she trusted him enough to follow his instructions. That womanly instinct thing again. God knows, it had to be something like that, because no woman in her right mind would swallow all he'd sprung on her in the past twenty-four hours.

Ellen trudged upstairs. She refused to cry. Pete would be upset enough without her falling apart, too. Standing near the foot of the stairs, the three men conferred quietly. She tried to listen in, but they might as well be speaking in Swahili for all she could understand.

"Is the kid going to be a problem?" Flynt murmured when the woman disappeared into one of the upstairs rooms.

Spence shook his head. "Best-case scenario, he won't even wake up. I can scoop him up in his blanket and carry him out to the car, and by the time he wakes, Ellen can hand him a fishing pole."

Flynt raised his eyebrows. "How old is this kid?"

"Unfortunately, he's too old, not to mention too smart, not to want some answers."

The words hadn't left his mouth before a sleepy Pete Wagner, wearing a rumpled pair of pajamas, appeared at the head of the stairs. "My mom says we're going somewhere." It was an accusation.

Spence waited until he was halfway up the stairs to answer. "Pete, something's come up. Awhile ago I remembered who I am and where I was going, and right now, I need you and your mom to help me out."

He was getting nowhere, that much was obvious by the sullen look on the boy's face. Funny, he'd never noticed it before, but Pete definitely had his mother's jawline. "Just tell me one thing...do you trust me?"

It took all of ten seconds—ten seconds they didn't have to spare. Pete nodded. "Yeah...I guess. Yeah."

"Okay, then, go scoop up whatever you'll need for the next few days and be down here in three minutes, you got that?"

"Do I have to take my schoolbooks?"

One of the men shook his head, the other one chuckled. Spence said, "Wouldn't hurt to toss 'em in. Don't forget to bring a few comic books, though, in case you get tired of fishing."

"Fishing?" Pete's eyes widened.

"Go, man! Two minutes and counting."

Ellen could hear Pete in his own room. Lord knew what he was packing. All his model planes, probably. She called softly from her room to his, "Don't forget your sweater and slippers."

Spence had called their temporary lodgings a shack. Not a cabin or a cottage, but a shack. She hoped it had running water.

Oh, Lord, what had she gotten herself involved in? She should have left the darn man where she'd found him instead of dragging him home with her.

Pete came in and dropped his backpack and a stack of schoolbooks beside the door. "Mom, do I really have to take my schoolbooks? I don't have room in my bag."

Quickly, she sorted through the stack, handed him two and said, "The others can wait. Did you bring another pair of shoes?"

"My black boots are on the back porch. Why do we have to go? Won't Miss Sara need us?"

While she finished packing, Ellen answered the questions she could and postponed the ones she didn't know the answers to. "Did you bring a change of underwear?"

"The ones without holes that I got for my birthday. Is Spence going to stay with us?"

Her hands stilled on the suitcase she was latching shut. "I don't know. Hon, he's probably got a lot to do now that he knows who he is and where he belongs."

And who belongs to him.

Ellen watched as Pete digested the information. Then he said, "But what about Miss Sara? She might not know how to have a baby by herself."

Relieved at not having to explain Spence's recovery, she said, "Moxie did just fine by herself. Miss Sara will come through like a champion—and this time, maybe we'll get a little girl. Now, if you're sure you've got everything you'll need, we'd better go."

"'Kay." He shrugged into his backpack and picked up the schoolbooks. "Mom, girl babies are called fillies."

Ellen took it as a good sign. At least he'd stopped asking unanswerable questions. She veered into the bathroom again on her way downstairs and grabbed her shampoo. She wasn't sure what a fishing shack would offer in the way of amenities, but it couldn't be much.

It wasn't much. Other than cane poles, spinning rods and two overflowing tackle boxes, the unpainted board-and-batten cabin offered a flyspecked, three-year-old calendar, some stained plastic dinnerware, a coffeepot and three cast-iron frying pans. The furniture could best be described as early utilitarian; a mixture of plastic and wooden porch furniture, for the most part, with a few yard-sale leftovers. Other than that, there were two bunk beds, a wood-burning stove, a two-burner gas range and a refrigerator that held one empty ice tray and three dead roaches.

Spence had explained that if she needed anything at all—if she heard or saw anything that bothered her, she was to scream her head off, that help was only a few yards away.

If he'd wanted to frighten her, that had done the job. Up until now everything had moved so quickly that she hadn't had time to think about the situation in which she found herself. It had been Donita who had suggested she take along a couple of pillows, sheets and light blankets.

Surprisingly enough, she'd instinctively liked the pair who'd been delegated to stay at the ranch. No sooner had they been introduced than Jose had tugged at his hat brim and headed back out to the barn to oversee Miss Sara's lying-in. Donita, whose barrel-racing days must be far in the past judging by her well-rounded figure, had been given a quick tour of the house. Both, Ellen had noted with shock, wore small sidearms under lightweight twill jackets.

"Don't you worry about this place, ma'am. Your horses, they'll be just fine. Jose'll look after them like they were his own babies."

And with that, she had to be satisfied.

The sun had risen in a blaze of glory shortly after they'd gotten under way, lending a further air of unreality to the whole crazy scenario. They had circled north of Mission Creek, with Spence driving Ellen and Pete in one SUV and the other two men following some distance back in the other.

"You realize I'll be without transportation?" Ellen had left the keys to both trucks with Jose and Donita.

"You won't be going anywhere, not without one of us," Spence had told her. He'd fallen silent then. In the pink light of dawn, he'd looked tense, worried. After the first few attempts she had given up trying to communicate. Pete had fallen asleep in the back seat, and Ellen had leaned over and covered him with one of the two blankets she'd brought along.

They had pulled up in front of a shack that looked as run down as all the others, including the ramshackle pier leading from the porch to the pond. Flynt and Tyler had pulled in right behind them, and two men emerged from the shacks on either side of the one she was expected to inhabit. Graying, nondescript men wearing baggy jeans and windbreakers, they'd been introduced as Beau and Melvin. Frick and Frack, she'd amended silently, knowing she would never be able to keep them apart in her mind.

"They're here if you need them. If they go fishing, it'll be from the pier where they can keep an eye on things. If you need groceries, make a list. One of them will run into town.''

That was it? she'd wanted to ask. After all we've been to each other?

Oh, God, you're pathetic, woman!

The leave-taking had been public. A few feet away, Tyler kept glancing at his watch while Flynt conferred quietly with Frick and Frack. Spence, too, had obviously been chaffing at the bit to leave, and Ellen told herself that after being away from his friends for two weeks, it was perfectly understandable.

But still she thought now, standing alone as she watched the sun glint off the forty-five acre pond, he could have taken her aside. He could have reached out and touched her face or her hand. He could have said he'd see her in a day or so. He could at least have said—

''Mom, what do catfish eat?'' Pete asked, interrupting her unrewarding thoughts.

''I don't know. Worms? Bugs?''

''I think they'd pro'ly eat chicken bits, don't you?'' They had stopped at a twenty-four-hour fast-food place and Spence had gone inside, emerging a few minutes later with several sacks of chicken nuggets, biscuits with and without ham and eggs, French fries, a carafe of coffee and a gigantic paper cup of iced orange juice.

''We'll get you more provisions later on today, including a cell phone and a list of numbers where you can reach us at any time,'' he'd said just before he'd taken his leave earlier that morning.

She had pinned her hopes on the promise, but it wasn't Spence who'd showed up with the cell phone and a box of supplies, it was the man called Flynt. ''I don't know how much Spence told you about what's going on, Ms. Wagner, but it'll help a whole lot if you can stay here for the next few days. The last thing he needs with things the way they are is to be worried about your safety."

Ellen had bridled at the implication that she was a drag on anyone, but decided there was no point in taking it up with this man. "A few days?" She knew from past experience that a few days could mean anything from a few hours to a few months. Without having her own transportation, leaving would not be easy. She would have to call a taxi, and she wasn't even sure how to tell them to find the place.

Besides, she wasn't at all certain her two watchdogs would allow her to leave. They looked like a couple of harmless old men on a fishing vacation, but looks could be deceiving.

"We'll be just fine," she'd assured the handsome, solemn-faced man with the piercing blue eyes. "You can tell Spence that he doesn't need to worry about us. We're perfectly capable of looking after ourselves."

He'd taken a moment to think it over, then shook his head. "One of us will be in touch as soon as anything changes. Meanwhile, if you think of anything you need—anything at all—just ask Beau or Melvin."

"Frick or Frack."

It took him a moment, but he'd almost smiled. "Right. Look, you've got your cell phone now, and the list of numbers. I'd appreciate it if you didn't call except in case of an emergency. The calls can't be traced the way landlines can, but with some pretty simple equipment, they can be intercepted."

Merciful heaven, what on earth had she gotten herself mixed up in? Ellen thought now. She didn't mind so much for herself—being an army wife had been more than a rude awakening; in the case of a spoiled debutante playing at being a college student, it had been a crash course in reality. But now she had Pete, and if anything happened to him, she would take on the so-called Texas Mafia herself. They didn't know what trouble was until they ran head-on into a mother's rage.

In the center of town, three men, two of them wearing headsets, waited in a van walled with electronic equipment. "Anything yet?" Spence whispered tersely. So far they had heard only the sounds of cursing, the scratch of a match, and the opening and closing of a drawer—probably a desk drawer. "Why the hell couldn't we get three sets of phones?"

"Lucky to get this much," Tyler muttered. He'd been the one to requisition the van. Tyler's specialty was disarming bombs, not procuring surveillance equipment. Fortunately, all three men, having been members of Special Forces, knew more than enough to get the job done.

Surveillance required patience, though, and patience at this point was in short supply. They were so close to the end of the game—that is, they were if everything fell into place as expected.

"I wish I knew what the hell we were waiting for," Tyler muttered.

"I can't tell you. I've been out of the loop too long, but I'll know it when I hear it." Occupied with another matter, neither Flynt nor Tyler had been in a position to get a lead on what was happening now that the new D.A. had been appointed.

"Then get on with it while I go get us some coffee and doughnuts."

Just then Tyler raised a hand for silence and leaned closer to the monitoring device. He ripped off his headset and fiddled with a control as a strident voice filled the overheated space.

"—know why? Because nobody trusts you anymore, that's why! Me, they can trust! I got a record to back me up. You? All you got is a two-bit contracting company!"

"That's Del Brio," Flynt confirmed. Another voice came into play and all three men stiffened.

"That's Ricky," Spence whispered. "See if you can bring it in better."

"Damn freakin' equipment. I told them I needed—"

"Hush!" Spence moved in closer to the speaker, concentrating on the tinny, static-filled conversation.

"If you'd stayed tight with your buddies, I wouldn't be in this fix, damn it! I'm working blind here, and you're not—"

"What the hell did you expect? For all I knew, they were responsible for my sister's—"

"They got off, didn't they?"

There was some highly inventive cursing followed by a sound as if one of the men had slammed a drawer shut. Then Del Brio's distinctive voice was heard again. "Forget Harrison. One way or the other, he's out of the picture now. Your other two friends are too worried about Callaghan to make trouble now. As for Haley, I been hearing things—"

"What things? Damn it, don't jerk me around like this, Frankie!"

The mob boss's voice took on a patently false geniality. "Way I hear it, your sister might still be alive. Now I'm not saying for sure, and I'm not saying I'm still interested in marrying her, I just happened to come into some information—"

"What information? What the hell are you talking about? We both know Haley's—'

"Take your hands off my shirt, boy." All signs of geniality, false or otherwise, disappeared. "Now, you want to work with me, or did you just come here to stir up trouble?"

Time passed slowly. At first Ellen was reluctant for Pete to go outside, but after the first few hours, she relented. There was no TV, no books—nothing at all to read other than schoolbooks and the comic books he'd brought with him, a few tattered fishing magazines and a copy of *Playboy,* which she quickly stashed inside the wood-burning stove.

Schoolbooks, Pete informed her, didn't count.

"Mom, I'm, hungry again. What are we having for lunch?"

"Let's see…we have canned corned-beef hash, canned tomatoes, a loaf of bread and some sandwich makings." Either Spence's friends were extremely unimaginative or they were unused to buying their own groceries.

"We could eat fish," Pete offered hopefully.

"So bait up and start fishing." She figured as long as he was entertained, he wouldn't worry about Miss Sara and her baby. Although the couple they'd left behind at the ranch had seemed competent enough, things could go wrong even in the best of circumstances.

"Yeah!" Pete shouted softly.

He was being forced to miss school. That put this in

the category of a vacation, and vacations were always welcome. If life as an army wife had taught her some basic lessons, being an army brat had been a good learning experience for her son. It had definitely helped make him more adaptable.

Lord, she loved Pete so much it hurt. He was still a child, but he considered himself the man of the family now, and as such, he took his duties seriously. Too seriously, sometimes, but there was nothing she could do about that. For a little while she'd thought that Spence might—

Forget it, she chided silently. Whatever Spence was involved in, it was big. Comparatively speaking, life on a struggling ranch—a horse breeding operation with two mares, two geldings and a bad-tempered stallion— was small. Too small to interest a man with an important position in town, and friends who could call in favors at the drop of a hat.

She could have cried, only it wouldn't have helped. Besides, Pete would have wanted to know why she was crying, and she could hardly tell an eight-year-old boy that she'd fallen head over heart in love with a man she had pulled out of a ditch.

Thirteen

Pete didn't catch any fish. If he was disappointed, he didn't let it show. Neither of them had ever dressed a fish before, but Ellen was sure she could have figured it out. "Maybe tomorrow," she consoled. "I've always heard that fish bite best early in the morning."

"Yeah, they pro'ly wake up hungry just like I do. Mom, do we have any cookies left?"

Without the regimen of school and chores to shape his days Pete was always hungry. She felt the opposite, having to force herself to eat.

That evening for supper, using two leftover biscuits, a can of tomatoes and whatever seasoning was on hand, Ellen made tomato pudding, one of her mother's favorite dishes to serve with the canned corned-beef hash. Her father used to turn up his nose and make some disparaging remark about taking the girl out of the country but not being able to take the country out of the girl.

"This tastes funny," Pete said.

"Then laugh, but don't complain unless you're ready to take over as chef-in-chief."

"Chef-in-chief, that's funny!"

She playfully cuffed him on the head. "Everything's funny to you."

Pete scraped his plate clean while Ellen told him stories of the people she'd known when she was a little girl, exaggerating facial expressions and accents, shamelessly throwing in outrageous details. By the time she ran out of imagination, he was asleep on the sagging sofa.

She covered him and left him there, then opened the door and stared out at the golden trail across Greasy Pond, compliments of the rising full moon. The scrubby oaks and cottonwoods cast romantic shadows on the row of weathered old shacks, disguising their dilapidated condition. Other than small birds skimming over the water, feeding on insects, nothing stirred.

And that, she supposed, was good.

Sooner or later Spence had to call. She didn't care if the call could be intercepted or not, she needed to hear his voice. Needed to know he hadn't forgotten her. Had whatever happened between them been only gratitude on his part for pulling him out of that ditch? Or on hers, for saving her son? She refused to believe that. She knew very well what her own feelings were; it was Spence's feelings she couldn't be sure of, didn't dare allow herself to believe.

Turning back inside, she knew she would never be able to sleep. What on earth was she supposed to do? How long were they going to be stuck there? If she'd had any cleaning supplies, she might even have given the place a thorough scrubbing. Anything was better than waiting and not knowing. Minute by minute, hour by hour, hoping for the best, expecting the worst.

Waiting for a call that didn't come.

So maybe when this was all over she would go back to Austin for a visit. Her father might even have mellowed with time, and Pete really did need a man in his life. A male role model. Right now all she had to offer was Booker and Clyde, and her father was definitely

better than that. It wouldn't hurt for Pete to be exposed
to a little refinement.

Spence's downtown office had been locked once
he'd been declared missing, but not before his files had
been searched for anything pertaining to the trial of
Alex Black. It had never occurred to him when he'd
locked the door behind him that morning nearly three
weeks ago, to remove the files directly pertaining to
the trial. Malone would have laid claim to all that his
first day in office.

As for tangential information that was far more potentially explosive, Spence had his own methods of
handling the paper trail that led from certain politicians,
plus a few of Mission Creek's big businessmen, directly to the Texas Mafia. If he'd known he was going
to turn up missing, he might have done a better job of
securing it, but he was hoping his hide-in-plain-sight
method had worked.

Missing. That was the official designation. Pressure
would have been brought to bear to declare him not
only missing but presumed dead, in which case everything in his office would have been subject to intense
scrutiny. Without a body, however, the police were
obliged to follow certain procedures. Any cop who
tried to rush the process would have tripped too many
alarms.

Still, pressure had to have been brought to bear by
certain individuals on certain others. Spence knew who
had done the applying; that was an open secret. What
he couldn't be sure of, not without further proof, was
just where that pressure had been applied. Who had
buckled? Had it been a top-down decision, or a bottom-
up one?

Del Brio's first act on taking over as the new mob boss had been to ramrod his man into the position of acting D.A. to rush through the trial before new evidence could be admitted. Shortly before he'd gone missing, Spence had been close to compiling enough evidence to rock a few well-placed citizens off their perches. He'd wanted that deposition for a turnkey job, but even without that he had enough to hand over to the feds. Let the attorney general's office take over. The evidence he'd compiled, if it was still where he'd left it in his office, was enough to build a solid case, even without the coup de grace.

Spence had wanted to go directly to his apartment after leaving Ellen and Pete in safe hands. He'd wanted to change into his own clothes, his own boots.

But in case the place was being watched, he'd sent Tyler in with a list.

Flynt drove him to a rundown motel out near the rodeo arena, where he registered using the name Jason Hale.

"ID?" the sleepy-eyed clerk had mumbled.

"Sorry. My wallet got lifted. I borrowed enough from a friend to live on for a few days, though."

"Be forty-five a day in advance, sign here."

Spence signed, using a slashing backhand. He counted out enough for three days, not that he intended to stay that long, but he'd just as soon not have to spend much time in the lobby. Considering the seedy clientele, it was just the sort of place where he might come face to face with Peaches and Silent Sal.

Inside the room, Flynt glanced around and said, "Did that clerk say forty-five a night or four-fifty an hour?"

"Go to hell," Spence retorted, a tired grin removing the bite from the words.

"Look, I'll have a driver's license for you in a few hours. Sure Jason Hale suits you?"

"Yeah, I'll stick with it until this mess is cleared up. I'm going to need wheels. It'll be a while before I can get in touch with my insurance company."

"I'll have a rental outside your door as soon as we get you documented."

"Tinted glass."

"You got it. But watch out, okay? We don't know how many people are still looking for you."

Spence stroked his bristly jaw. He'd gone without shaving since yesterday. Another couple of days and it would take a Weed Eater to mow his beard.

Seeing the gesture, Flynt warned him not to shave. "You're looking just crummy enough to escape notice."

"Thanks," Spence said dryly, and of all things, he thought of Ellen. Of the carefully controlled look on her face when she'd brought him her husband's shaving gear. Had he read more into the simple gesture than she'd intended? At the time he'd still been pretty groggy.

He had some unfinished business to deal with where Ellen Wagner was concerned, but before he could do anything about it, he had to wind up what he'd started here in town. What happened after that would be up to her. And Pete.

He knew what he wanted to happen.

For the next few hours, holed up in a crummy little motel room with mustard-yellow walls, a rose-colored bedspread and a few faded rodeo posters, Spence wrote down every scrap of information he could remember, including where the hard evidence was located, its source and how it all tied together. He drew diagrams. It helped him to think more clearly—helped to prevent him from busting out, heading downtown and making a royal ass of himself. And in the process, ruining whatever chance he had of pulling this case together in time to hand it off to the FBI. Alex Black was going to take the fall—there wasn't much he could do about that now, but hell, the guy had pulled the trigger. Judge Bridges hadn't been his first hit. As young as he was, Black had been no amateur.

Only if Spence could make his case tight enough and hand it off to the feds would all the dominoes come tumbling down. Justice would be served in the long run—or as much of it as any man could expect.

God, he sounded jaded. Time he got out of this rat race.

He had his own ranch—had he thought to tell Ellen? Not that he'd had much time even to visit for the past couple of years. Hers was small; his was even smaller, but his was a lot better managed. Maybe something could be worked out between them, although they were separated by practically the entire width of Lone Star County.

From time to time, to ease the tension gathering at the base of his neck, he flopped back on the sagging mattress and stared at the stained acoustical-tiled ceiling. He pictured another bedroom—paneled walls, white cotton curtains—nothing fancy, but clean and comfortable and somehow just right.

He pictured a woman standing beside the bed in a white chenille bathrobe with the sash pulled tight, revealing the flare of her hips, the narrowness of her waist. Fresh from her bath, her face would be flushed, her hair tousled and still damp. "Ellen, Ellen," he murmured. "What are we going to do? How the devil are we going to work things out?"

They met at the courthouse. Spence had set the time for three hours past midnight, knowing that traffic would be practically nonexistent, security at its most lax. At this point, he couldn't afford to trust even the cleaning crew. While Tyler distracted the lone security guard, the other two men slipped up the back stairway and into the office that still bore Spence's name in gold letters on the pebbled-glass door. Thank God they hadn't yet got around to declaring him officially out of the picture or the locks would have been changed, his office space reassigned.

"I hear Malone got the big corner office," Tyler said quietly, referring to the newly appointed district attorney.

"Southwestern exposure. Once he finds out the place is an oven eight months out of the year he might change his mind. Look in the top file drawer under Insurance."

"Insurance?"

"What, you expected a folder labeled Corruption In Internal Affairs And Business Ties To The Mob?"

Flynt pulled the thick file while Tyler cleared a working space, then the two men began scanning the contents. The papers at the front and the back of the folder concerned insurance. The rest did not.

"Damn, just look at this," Tyler said softly.

Flynt glanced up from his own stack of paper—more interesting reading—then glanced over his shoulder to where Spence sat hunched over his desktop computer.

The three men worked feverishly. From time to time,

one of them would utter a quiet oath. Flynt read a certain document and whistled softly just as Spence shut down his computer and turned away. "Yeah, sort of gets you right here, doesn't it?" He slapped a hand over his heart.

"Man, this is going to blow this county wide open."

"Let's hope so. Grab the whole folder and let's get out of here before Gus makes another round."

At the sound of a phone, all three men jumped. Spence stared at the instrument on his desk. No lights were blinking.

"Mine," Tyler acknowledged. Hips braced against the long oak table that had been part of the original courthouse furnishings dating from the early 1920s, he spoke quietly. "Murdoch. Yeah, go on, I'm listening." He swore, and then said, "I'll be there as soon as— Look, give me twenty-four hours. I'll get word to you as soon as I know our E.T.A." A long pause and then, "Two, possibly three. Meet us at the embassy. And keep me posted on any change of plans, will you?"

Turning to the other two men, he said, "If we've got everything we need here, I suggest we get moving. That was my contact with military intelligence. Spence, I'll bring you up to date since you've been out of the loop, but it'll have to be the condensed version." He began gathering up file folders, shoving them into a battered briefcase. "I told you Luke's located the commander, but before he could extract him, things blew wide open. Literally. Luke got a face full of shrapnel. He's in a makeshift field hospital somewhere in the jungles of Central America. Surgery took place a couple of hours ago." He looked at one man, then the other. "My contact says the prognosis doesn't look too promising."

Spence froze. "But he came through surgery?"

"Yeah, he's stabilized for the time being, but it looks like he might not regain his sight."

All three men fell silent. It was impossible to think of their friend being blind. Luke Callaghan was a V.M.I. classmate, a fellow Gulf War veteran. A loner in spite of his wealth, Luke permitted very few people to get close to him. Spence, Flynt, Tyler—and one other man—were among the chosen few.

"Come on, let's get out of here," Flynt said gruffly. "We've got plans to make, places to go and things to do. Man, I hope your passport wasn't in your car when you tangled with that twister."

"Office safe at home. Why?"

"We'll swing by and pick it up. Anything else we can grab later."

"You want to clue me in?" Spence went about opening shades and switching off lights, leaving things the way they'd found them. Until they were ready to spring the trap, he was still officially missing.

Day two was exactly like day one at the catfishing resort known as Greasy Pond. Pete fished, using bait provided by one of their guardian angels. Wieners, in this case. Yesterday's bait had been chicken nuggets. Ellen had gone to the manager and borrowed a child-size life preserver and made him wear it, much to his disgust. "Mom, I'm just going to sit on the end of the pier."

"You might fall off."

"No, I won't, and anyway, I can swim real good."

"Oh? And just where did you learn how to swim?" She had thought more than once about her father's Olympic-size swimming pool, not to mention all the other advantages Leonard Summerlin could have provided.

"I know you hold your breath and kick and do your arms like this." Scrawny arms flying, he demonstrated. "'Sides, there was this TV show about lifeguards and all, and they used these things to hold on to and kicked real hard—I think it was called *Bayside,* or something like that. Anyhow, these guys were real cool. Maybe I could be a lifeguard when I grow up."

Closing her eyes, Ellen shook her head slowly from side to side. *Baywatch?* Her son watched that beach bunny parade and thought the guys were cool?

She'd have to monitor his viewing more carefully.

There were few people around. From time to time she saw the men who were supposed to be her security. If they'd deliberately tried to look anonymous, they couldn't have succeeded better. But of course, that was the whole idea of surveillance. It was supposed to be discreet.

She wondered where Spence was now. Sitting on the porch, leaning back against the weathered, sun-warmed plank wall, she watched her son concentrate intently on fishing for catfish in a muddy pond and thought about the man who had impacted her life with the force of a meteor. The man she had fallen in love with against her better judgment.

Logic told her she didn't know him well enough to be in love with him, but since when had logic played a part in her life? Little more than a dozen years ago she'd been an inexperienced, overprivileged student in an all-girl school, with a safe, comfortable future all mapped out for her. That had ended the day she'd fallen in love with a soldier.

Now, having finally managed to put away her grief

and inch forward with her life again, she had made the mistake of falling for a man without a name, a man without a past, thinking that he would be hers alone because he had nowhere else to go, no one to go back to.

Delusional. No other word to describe it, she told herself with a smile that held more sadness than bitterness. Some women learned from experience; others never did. Jake had been the best thing that had ever happened to her. He'd given her Pete and more joy than she would ever have known with someone like Greg Sanders.

And what had Spence Harrison offered her?

Two nights of unimaginable bliss followed by a vacation she didn't want and didn't have time for in a place she would never have chosen in a million years, plus far too much time to wallow in hindsight.

She slapped at a deer fly hovering around her shoulder. With Christmas coming on fast, she would do better to start thinking of how she was going to manage to buy Pete both a new bike and a puppy. If her son had truly been matchmaking, as Spence had hinted, he was going to be sorely disappointed, because sooner or later all this cloak-and-dagger stuff would end and they would go back home. And she'd be right back where she'd been before Spence had tumbled into her life. Staving off bankruptcy while she tried to absorb a crash course in managing a breeding operation. Trying to be a good mother and make up for Pete's not having a father.

So what was she doing stuck out in the middle of nowhere in a shack that barely had indoor plumbing, while a pair of strangers took over her house and the delivery of another foal? The woman who was now living in her house, washing her dishes and cooking food from her freezer, wore a gun strapped to her hip, of all bizarre things.

Just when, Ellen asked herself, had her life turned into one of those made-for-TV melodramas? More to the point, what would happen in the next act? A daring rescue by the Texas Rangers? A midnight raid by the mob?

Not if she had anything to say about it. Once before she had taken control of her life; she could do it again. She would give him three days, starting with yesterday, and then she was leaving, even if she had to hitch a ride with the meter-reader all the way back home.

They met in one of the smaller private rooms at the club. Flynt had ordered three grilled sirloins brought in, then dismissed the waiter with a large tip. A few minutes later Tyler and Spence slipped in through a service entrance. "Thought you might be hungry by now," Flynt said, his usually somber expression momentarily lighting. "This might have to last us awhile."

"Thanks. Room service at the Bucking Bronco Motel runs to candy bars, bagged snacks and lukewarm colas."

Over huge, sizzling platters, the three men quickly got down to business. "I've lined up a charter for—" Tyler checked his watch "—three hours from now. That doesn't give us much time. Spence, you're sidelined on this mission. From what I've seen so far today, you've got more than enough to take to the FBI. Once it's in their jurisdiction, you can collect your lady and stand by because we'll need someone on this end. I'm not sure what we'll run into down there."

Spence nodded, and the other man continued to speak. "I don't know the latest on Westin's situation—my contact lost touch three days ago. Once we get word, we'll figure out how to deal with it, but right now, Luke's our main concern."

"Can he travel?" Flynt poured more water from the frosted pitcher.

"Barely. But he'll be better off almost anywhere than in a field hospital in some Central American jungle. With any luck, we'll be able to fly him back to the States."

Luke, severely injured, maybe blind? And he couldn't even take part in the rescue mission? Spence dropped his knife and fork with a clatter, his appetite gone. As much as he hated to admit it, Tyler was right. As in any covert mission, the fewer men who went in, the less the chance of discovery. "You'll need backup," he said. "Two going in—three would be even better if you're going to have a chance at pulling off a clean extraction."

"Right. Unfortunately, the hornet's nest you've stirred here has to be brought under control as quickly as possible, and you're the only one who can do it. Your timing sucks, old buddy." Tyler summed up the situation with his usual precision.

"I'm thinking we might want to bring Ricky in on this," Flynt said thoughtfully.

"Mercado! Are you crazy?" Tyler shoved back his chair and began pacing. "He's the last thing we need. We've got one good shot at getting Luke out of there while the military goes in after the commander. I'm going in. I know the territory."

"And I'm in," said Flynt immediately.

"Don't count on it," Tyler retorted. "Hang loose

until we know what it will take to get to that field hospital. We might end up short of space, depending on how much medical personnel Luke needs to make the flight.''

It was Spence who cast the tie-breaking vote. ''I say Flynt stays here as backup in case I'm tied up and you need help on this end. Ricky's done missions with us before. He was one of the team until Haley disappeared.'' Luke, Flynt, Spence and Tyler had all been implicated in the disappearance of their friend's sister. Even after they'd been cleared, the breach had remained.

Flynt picked up the summary. ''Look, we know Mercado's a good man to have in a tight spot, he proved that in Desert Storm. Right now he's just lost a battle with Del Brio for control of the mob, so he's looking to prove something. You want to know what I think? I think he never really wanted to head up the mob. It was because Rick didn't want Haley getting mixed up with Del Brio. At least, that's what started it. If I'm right, this might be a good time to bring him back into the fold.''

Tyler nodded thoughtfully. ''And get him out of town before he ticks off the wrong guys. Okay, I'll go along with it. I'll give him a call right now.''

Flynt glanced at his watch again. ''You'll need to bring him up to speed in a hurry, though, if you're going to fly south in a few hours.''

Ellen couldn't wait any longer. Food supplies had been delivered each day by one of the two bewhiskered guardian angels. ''I want you to call me a taxi,'' she said to the one she thought of as Frack. ''Nobody's looking for me, and I really do need to go home. My mares are right in the middle of foaling.''

"Now, ma'am—"

"Either you call me a cab or I'll hitchhike."

"Now, ma'am—" The poor man tried again, but Ellen knew how to put her foot down and make it stick. She wasn't, after all, a criminal. Legally, there was no way they could keep her here against her will without risking a kidnaping charge.

"Ma'am, I'll take you home, but we'll have to let Mr. Harrison know. He's not gonna like it."

"Go right ahead. You call anyone you need to call, but I'm going home."

Fourteen

Back at the Bucking Bronco Motel a short while later, Spence peered through the Venetian blinds to see an old man stringing a row of Christmas lights from post to post outside the shabby stuccoed building. He came to a burned-out bulb, spat a stream of tobacco juice and began to swear.

"Don't sweat it, old man," Spence muttered. "There are worst things in life than a burned-out bulb." Closing the blinds against the low December sun, he yawned. He needed to sleep while he could, there might not be time later.

He had almost reached the stage of utter relaxation, his mind seeming to float somewhere over his head, when the phone rang. It was Flynt, calling to report that Tyler and Ricky had got off on schedule. "As soon as we know anything about Luke's condition, I'll be setting up things here so that if he can't make it home yet, Michael can be in touch via computer. Thank God for technology!" Michael O'Day was a top-notch surgeon as well as a good friend.

"Technology won't be much help against biology. Some of those jungle viruses aren't even in the books yet."

"Evidently the medics knew enough to patch him up. Let's hope they knew enough to wash their hands first. I'll keep you posted as soon as I get another report."

Spence flexed his shoulders, sat up and rubbed his burning eyes. "How did Ricky strike you? Is he back on track?"

"I'd lay odds on it. He seemed genuinely affected when Tyler described the situation. Offered to ride shotgun on this mission, and then to go back in to try to get Westin out."

"Alone?"

"Working single-handed, with the military, or with any of us."

"Boy needs a hobby," Spence said dryly. Unfortunately, his mob-connected family was trying hard to provide one. "Well, you know where I am if you need me. Damn! Of all times to be out of circulation!"

"Don't screw up now, friend. You're too close to wrapping things up. Judging from what I saw last night, you're going to have your hands full any minute now. I told Michael to hold off making any definite arrangements. Best-case scenario, they'll be bringing him home, but things don't always work out the way we plan."

"You got that right. While they're on the scene, maybe they can get a lead on whether or not the commander's been moved." Both men fell silent, thinking of the man who had once risked his life for theirs.

"By the way," Flynt said, his voice carefully noncommittal. "Ricky's got some screwy idea about Haley's still being alive. Remember that conversation we overheard between him and Del Brio?"

"Haley…God, that seems like ancient history now, so much has happened since then."

"It's still happening, my friend," Flynt said with a

trace of wry humor that had been buried deeply for too many years. "Hang tight, I'll keep you posted."

Exhausted from going without sleep for too long, Spence had just dozed off when the phone rang again. Groaning, he sat up, rubbed his eyes hard with his fists and reached for the instrument. "Yeah, Ha—" Hale or Harrison? "I'm here, go ahead."

"Mr. Harrison, this is Beau out at Greasy Pond. I just took your woman home. She was cutting up something fierce, said if I didn't take her she was gonna hitchhike. I knowed you wouldn't want that."

Spence felt the beginnings of a headache. He was too old for this life-on-the-edge stuff. Somewhere along the line he'd lost his taste for adrenaline. "Yeah, you did the right thing, Beau. How'd everything look around her place? Did you check it out?"

"Some lady wearing an apron over a sidearm opened the door. Made me come in for a cup of coffee and a plate o' something that like to burnt the hair off'n my tongue. Your lady and the kid headed directly for the barn, so I took a good look around while I was there. Guy up on a big bay stallion, come down to talk to the lady. Figgered he was one o' your folks."

"You figured right. Jose's a retired Texas Ranger. The woman is his wife."

"Your lady said she was some kind of a horse breeder."

"Small time…just starting out." Spence had long since concluded that Ellen was no natural when it came to horses. He gave her credit for hanging in there, though.

"Figgered," the old man said drolly.

Spence thanked him, pulled both men off duty and said he'd be in touch. They were from a mom-and-pop security firm he used occasionally, having found them completely trustworthy, if somewhat unorthodox.

"Ellen, Ellen, what am I going to do about you?" he whispered softly. Now wide awake, he gave up on getting any sleep in the near future. Instead of calling her directly, he called Jose on his cell phone. "Anything going on there? Any strangers nosing around?"

"Couple of guys turned up, said they used to work here. They took off, no questions asked."

Which could mean almost anything, Spence thought. He asked Jose to stick around until further notice.

"We promised the grandkids we'd spend Christmas with them."

"No problem, it should just be a couple more days. I'll have you in Laredo in plenty of time to stuff stockings."

He hung up, yawning, rubbing his eyes, and headed for the shower. Christmas? Welcome to the real world, he thought wryly. In the real world he had an appointment to meet with an FBI agent out of Dallas in about forty-five minutes. After that, he'd be waiting to hear from Tyler or Ricky that they'd extracted Luke from the field hospital and that he was holding his own.

Which meant he wouldn't be getting much sleep anytime soon. A cold shower would have to serve. Hell, he couldn't even shave, and his beard was at the itchy stage.

In a small plane flying steadily over the mountainous terrain of the small Central American country of Mezcaya, having left the jungles behind, Tyler Murdoch's thoughts raced forward. They had hoped to fly directly back to the States, but Luke's condition was still too precarious to risk the longer flight. Instead, they were heading toward the city of San Salvador. Rick had radioed ahead to the hospital. By the time they landed, there should be an ambulance waiting at the airfield.

Tyler, tensely watching the level of IV fluids, tried not to allow the droning noise to dull his edge. He had a feeling his friend had been feigning sleep for the past few hours, but not until Ricky moved forward to join the pilot did Luke open his eyes. "There's a way," the injured man whispered, "to get the commander out." He closed his eyes again. Tyler, now fully alert, sensed there was more to come.

"Man on the flying trapeze. Ever hear...that old song?" Weakly, Luke indicated the swaying tubes hanging over him from the stands on either side. He was being monitored and medicated, even twenty-five hundred feet above mean sea level.

"Can't say I ever did. You can fill me in on what I need to know once we get you settled. Shouldn't be much longer now." It was hard to read an expression when three-quarters of a man's face was covered in bandages.

"Chopper. Swing in...swing out." Luke grimaced, his fingers clenching and unclenching at his side.

Tyler said gruffly, "Pipe down, friend, we'll talk about it later. Meanwhile, how about I bring you up to speed on what's been happening lately?"

"Yeah...you do that. Feels like I've been...gone a year, at least."

Tyler quickly changed his mind about revealing too much. His intention had been to distract, not to agitate. "Weather's been real funky. Had a hell of a rain a few weeks ago—couple of twisters came through, but didn't do much damage." Other than sidelining their friendly D.A. with a bad case of amnesia while Frank

Del Brio, the new mob boss, pulled in a few political favors designed to manipulate the justice system more to his liking. Hardly the kind of news designed to cheer up a man who'd just had a bomb go off in his face.

Tyler still didn't know the details of what had gone wrong with Luke's mission. Last he'd heard, they had a surefire plan for getting Phillip Westin out of the hands of the guerrillas. All that would have to wait, though, until Luke's prognosis looked a bit more hopeful. "I guess you don't know about Flynt's new family."

"Flynt? A family? What happened?" A glimmer of the old Luke came through despite the bandages and the pain medication.

"Well, there was this baby, see... We were playing one Sunday morning. Ninth tee. The usual foursome, only you weren't there, so we pulled in Michael O'Day. You know Michael."

"The family...you said Flynt's...got a new family."

Luke was tiring. The move had not been easy; they'd had to jog more than two miles over rough terrain, carrying him on a stretcher, to reach the clearing where the plane awaited. "Yeah, well, y'see, there was this baby in a basket. I mean, that's the last thing you expect to find on a golf course, right? A baby girl with a note on her. Wonder we didn't miss her."

Carefully monitoring the instruments, Tyler tailored the story to fit Luke's level of endurance. "She's a girl, like I said. Cute as a button. Flynt's got her, at least until we can figure out where she belongs."

Luke grinned, then began to chuckle, but broke off with a cough. Alarmed, Tyler gripped his hand. "Easy there, old buddy, we'll be on the ground in five minutes. Double that and we'll have you secured to a real bed instead of this stinking canvas contraption.''

After a moment Luke Callaghan started to speak, caught his breath, then tried again. "Did I ever tell you…about that night…''

"Shhh, it can wait. Hang on now, this field doesn't look like it's in great shape. Might be a rough landing.''

Luke felt hands gripping his shoulders, sensed when Ricky Mercado came back to help steady him for the landing. The medication was beginning to wear off. To counter the pain, Luke thought about the last time he had seen Ricky's sister, Haley.

It had been at a homecoming celebration for the 14th Marines. They'd all been celebrating a bit too much when someone had suggested a midnight boat ride. Had Haley been the first to climb aboard? Probably. There'd been something almost…brittle about her that night, or so it seemed now, looking back.

"Easy there, friend, we're almost down." Tyler's soothing voice reassured him even as his hands gripped his shoulders.

Luke closed his mind to the pain. He thought about that night at Lake Maria. He'd agreed to hold the celebration at his own estate. He remembered the laughter, the teasing, the flirting—the way they'd all piled into the small boat because Haley was there, and they'd all been in love with Haley, beautiful Haley Mercado.

That was the night she had disappeared. Drowned.

God, don't think about that, not now!

And so as he felt the flaps engage and the air speed begin to fall off, Luke thought instead of a night many months after they had been first charged, then eventually cleared, in the disappearance of the woman they'd all loved.

The Saddlebag, long a favorite watering hole, had been crowded that night. He'd needed a drink...needed something, anyway. He had found it in the person of a cool, beautiful blonde who had reminded him of—

But that was crazy. Haley was dead, they'd all known that.

All the same, there'd been something about the woman who'd refused to give him her name. Said she lived in London, and had come to the States on personal business.

Luke had not been interested in her business, only in her body. Maybe it had been the beers—he'd had a few more than his usual quota. Maybe it had been—

Hell, who knew why it had happened? All he'd known was that the lady had been more than willing— even eager—and he'd been more than ready to oblige. It occurred to him now that that was exactly the kind of encounter that could lead to giveaway babies like the one Flynt had reportedly found.

But he'd taken precautions...hadn't he? He always took precautions.

He frowned, trying to remember. Still, all he could recall was how much the woman had reminded him of Haley—something in the way she moved...

He was way off base here. There was no connection. All these medications he'd been given had messed up his mind. All the same, what if Haley had lived?

Then there would have been no mysterious blonde from London.

Man you've got to cut it out, Luke told himself.

He needed to focus on regaining his sight, because he still had some unfinished business back in that bug-ridden hellhole of a jungle prison camp. He would go back to Mission Creek to recuperate if that was what it took, but one way or another he was going to get the commander out of that stinking cell. He owed him that much and more.

The light plane touched down, bounced twice, then rolled to a halt. Before Luke could brace himself again, the doors opened and medics swarmed inside. Eyes closed, a smile on his face, he translated the words they spoke, which were the rough equivalent of, "There you go, sir, we've got you safe now."

"Mom, look at her, she knows me!" Pete was as excited over the new foal as he had been the first one. "Bowser likes her, too."

Miss Sara's little girl was called Brownie. Her papers and Bowser's papers would show something a bit more dignified in keeping with their lineage, which was respectable, if hardly spectacular. At least Ellen knew that much about registering the birth of her babies.

Seated on a three-legged stool, she worked at mending a bridle. It wasn't her favorite task, but like so many others, she'd learned to do it. Necessity brought out a surprising number of hidden talents.

"Boy, I wish Spence could see her. I bet he'd really like her."

Hearing the wistful note in her son's voice, Ellen laid aside the strap of worn leather and sighed. She had tried to explain that Spence was an important man, with a lot of important business that would have kept him too busy to contact them for these past few days. When she had tried to describe just what it was that a district attorney did, Pete had summed it up in his own terms. "Getting the bad guys."

It was as good a description as any.

Clyde and Booker had not been back. Jose had said before he and Donita left to spend the Christmas holidays with family in Laredo that he might be able to find a couple of reliable hands if Ellen didn't mind hiring old men.

At this point Ellen would have hired anything on two legs that could lift a bale of hay—or even a split bale.

"They're not real old, they're what you might called 'well seasoned.' Trouble is, most big outfits don't want geezers on the payroll. Claim they're not cost-effective."

"I can't offer health insurance, or even a place to stay. Meals, of course…"

"These guys are on Medicare, and if you don't mind, they could fix up a place in the tractor shed."

"Well, sure. I mean, I suppose so. They can work, can't they? I mean, they're not that old?"

Jose grinned, revealing a glint of gold. "No, ma'am, they're what you might call the perfect age. Got all the hell-raisin' out of their systems, now they're ready to settle down and work. Takes some longer than others to figure out that work's where a man finds real satisfaction."

So Ellen tentatively agreed to interview the two men who would be showing up sometime tomorrow. She wished she knew more about men in general. Wished Jose and Donita hadn't had to leave. Wished Spence had never recovered his memory and—

Oh, no, she didn't wish that. She had more than her share of shortcomings, but selfishness wasn't among them.

"Mom, if I get a dog for Christmas, could I call him Stormy?"

That was Pete. No beating around the bush, hinting at what Santa Claus might bring him. He was young for his age in some ways because she'd had a tendency to baby him, but at eight, he was too old for fairy tales. Ellen only wished she could make the same claim.

Actually, she'd just seen a cute puppy out at the pound yesterday. It would cost more than she could easily afford to get his shots brought up to date, as she'd just bought a practically new bike from the thrift shop, but when she'd seen the pup's funny face and that stub of a tail wagging madly, she'd fallen in love.

"Stormy it is, then. If we get a dog."

"Aw, Mom, I'm too old for surprises."

Ellen reached up and caught her son, tugging him down onto her lap. "You're ancient. You're so old you're getting mossy." She plucked a stalk of hay from Pete's hair and tickled him. He had grown up too quickly. She used to spend hours rocking him, singing—taking such comfort from the feel of his small, warm body. Jake had accused her of waking him from a sound sleep just to rock him, and she hadn't denied it.

She wouldn't trade a single moment of his childhood for any amount of treasure. He was all she had now, and they would do just fine. And if she spent a part of each night remembering—wishing for something more, then she could just *un*remember and *un*wish. Get real, as one of her friends from school used to say.

"Mom, do you know Spence's address? I made him a picture so he wouldn't forget us, but it doesn't have a frame or glass or anything, so we could mail it, couldn't we?" Pete's small face puckered into a frown. "Mom, did you get something in your eye? 'Cause I know how to get it out. See, you grab hold of your eyelashes on top and pull 'em down over the bottom ones, and it sort of squeezes out whatever's in there. I could help you if you want me to.''

Fifteen

On his own ranch some thirty-five miles north of town, Spence glanced around one last time. He'd been there for the past few days, after winding up his affairs in town. He was alone now, his housekeeper and manager having just left to do last-minute Christmas shopping. Elnora had packed what she called his survival kit, an assortment of holiday delicacies, for him to take with him. The pup was waiting for him outside, yapping her head off. He didn't know how much of that Ellen would put up with. The collie pup had seemed quiet at the pet shop.

His suitcase was ready, sitting beside the front door. He'd already packed more than enough for several days, including his best boots, his work boots and a pair of sneakers. He had no intention of stepping into Jake Wagner's shoes in any but the figurative sense.

He almost wished he'd waited on the packing, though. Maybe he was taking too much for granted, showing up on her doorstep, bag and baggage. For all he knew, she might consider herself well rid of him, considering she hadn't been too happy with the arrangements he'd made for her safekeeping.

"Nothing ventured, nothing gained," he said decisively as he scooped up the large box containing smoked turkey, sweet potato casserole, cookies, fruitcake and the world's richest chocolate pie, Elnora's specialty. One way or another, he told himself as he shifted the bike and the dog carrier to make room for the food box, things would work out. They had to, because a life without Ellen and Pete wasn't worth living.

What had that woman done to him? He asked himself for the hundredth time since he'd left her at a low-rent resort called Greasy Pond. He only hoped it worked both ways, because if it didn't, he had the case of his life to prove.

He should have called first. Should have called three days ago. After securing the bike so that it wouldn't topple over, the food box so that it wouldn't slide, he poked a treat through the gate of the dog carrier. "You're going to love these people, Lady," he said to the wistful canine face that peered through the wire at him.

Then, sliding in under the wheel, he dialed Ellen's number on his car phone. And listened while it rang, and rang, and rang. "Come on, sweetheart, answer the phone...tell me you're as eager to see me as I am to see you." She must be out in the barn. One of the first things he was going to do was run the phone line to the barn and into every room in the house, then buy her half a dozen cell phones if that was what it took to keep track of her.

He let it ring ten times. Okay, so he'd show up unannounced and play it by ear. Probably be better anyway—catch her off guard, before she had her defenses locked in place. He'd run into those defenses before and damned near come out a loser.

Without a backward glance, Spence Harrison drove away from the ranch he'd bought with the idea of retiring after a few more years to raise horses, play poker and undertake the occasional covert mission with his old friends should the occasion arise. But fighting corruption took a lot out of a man who wasn't getting any younger.

Spence knew he should have called Ellen to let her know he was coming. Not to ask permission, just to give her warning, in case she didn't want to see him again. But he'd been going flat-out for the past forty-eight hours, contacting the appropriate people and arranging to turn over the rest of the evidence he'd compiled against the mob, and then doing it. On top of that there had been the covert meetings, alerting key people that the new acting D.A. was corrupt and steering them in the direction of indisputable evidence.

Only when all that was done did he leave everyone from the attorney general on down in stunned disbelief by turning in his resignation, effective immediately. He'd cleared out his files, all the while networking with Tyler and Flynt as to Luke's condition and how best to effect the rescue of Commander Westin.

It occurred to him that, with the exception of those few weeks when he'd been out of circulation, he'd been going flat-out ever since Judge Bridges had managed to get him admitted to the Virginia Military Institute. God, that had been—how many years ago? The judge had threatened to toss him in the slammer and throw away the key if he got any grade below a B on a single course.

After that had come the military, the Gulf War, including captivity. Once he'd mustered out of the marines he'd gone after his law degree with an idea of repaying the judge for his unwavering faith.

During all that time, his personal life had been put

on hold. And now he desperately wanted a personal
life—a family, a home and a career that wasn't fueled
by caffeine and adrenaline.

Had he left it too late? For a supposedly intelligent
man, one who was widely known for his incisive in-
tellect and his delicate hand at negotiations, he might
have screwed this one up before he could even make
his case. If she said no, he was busted. Flat-out washed
up. Never in his life had he begged for anything, not
even when he'd been charged with reckless endanger-
ment after Haley had disappeared, supposedly drowned
when an overloaded boat full of beer-drinking revelers
had overturned in Luke's private lake one dark night.

He'd managed to get through that—they all had,
with the judge's help. God knows why, but the judge
had believed them—believed in them.

This time Spence was prepared to do whatever it
took. Bended knee—the whole routine. He'd bought a
ring. Nothing ostentatious because that wasn't Ellen's
style. For Pete he'd bought the pup and a bike that was
a little large for him now, but one he'd grow into.
Something to live up to, to look forward to—that was
important for kids. If he'd had a single goal back when
he was Pete's age other than being the biggest, toughest
rat in the pack, it might not have taken a head-on collision with the law to turn him around.

Rambling thoughts, increasingly tense, used up the
minutes as the miles flew past. Little had changed since
that day almost a month ago when his whole life had
been turned upside down in one split second. With the
window down, he sped past field after field of produce,
orchard after orchard of citrus fruit, and pasture after
pasture of beef cattle. The mingled smells of grass,
grapefruit and cattle manure was as good as it got, he

told himself. Mission Creek was a fine town, no better and probably no worse than any small town where bloodlines and blood feuds went back for generations. He wasn't a part of all that. Had been for a while—although not the bloodlines—but he wouldn't be sorry for a change of venue.

When he pulled into the yard, he realized things looked pretty much the same as when he'd left. Compared to his own small, well-managed operation, Ellen's place was downright shabby. Small house, attractive despite the chipped paint, the leaning antenna, the shaggy, overgrown shrubbery and patch of weeds out back that was supposed to have been a kitchen garden, only Ellen said she'd never had time to spend on it.

For a woman who had grown up in Ellen's circumstances, she had a pretty firm grip on reality. One of the first things Spence had done when he'd got back to town was check out Leonard Summerlin in case he suddenly needed to relocate Ellen and Pete. The report had summed him up as an international investment broker and aging playboy, recently remarried, reported to be undergoing treatment for prostate cancer. Evidently Summerlin had inherited money and used it to make more. Nothing wrong with that. He'd been a good parent as far as anyone knew, but a lousy role model. Whatever had happened between Ellen and her father—she'd told him some of it, but he had an idea there was more—Spence intended to do all he could to mend fences, especially now that the old man might be facing a challenge to his health. Knowing Ellen, she'd never forgive herself if her father died before she could forgive him.

But first he had a few fences of his own to mend.

* * *

They were gone. The first thought that ran through his mind when he knocked on the door a third time, rattled the knob and waited was that she'd already set out to mend her own fences by taking Pete to Austin for the holidays.

Instead of feeling glad, he felt betrayed.

He knocked again just to be sure. If she happened to be upstairs, she might not have heard him. He glanced toward the barn, saw that the horses were outside, the two foals with their dams in one pasture, separated from Zeus and the geldings.

She wouldn't go off and leave her stock untended, not the Ellen he knew. Nor would she have gone off and left Booker and Clyde to look after things. But, there was no sign of the small truck.

The duelly was there, however, parked beside the horse trailer. Rattling the door again, he yelled, "Ellen!"

Then he moved to the edge of the porch and called again, in case she happened to be in the backyard hanging clothes.

She wasn't there.

Suddenly he felt as if a cold north wind had just blown across his naked skin. Just because she wasn't here didn't mean anything had happened to her. The first thing he'd done was to make damn sure she was safe, especially after Beau had called to say she'd insisted on returning home.

But two nights ago one of Del Brio's hit men had been killed when his car had gone off the road at a high rate of speed. According to the EMT who was one of the first to arrive on the scene, the man had been covered with tattoos. Further checking indicated that Silent Sal had disappeared and was rumored to be headed south across the border. One of the new hires at the police department was checking into the case. Spence had met the detective and been favorably impressed.

"Ellen, where the hell are you?" he muttered now, more worried than he wanted to admit.

She was obviously away on some errand. A Christmas program at school, maybe at church. There was a wreath of fresh greenery on the door. He recognized Pete's artistic efforts. The plastic jet model didn't add a whole lot of color, but the effect was cheerful enough.

"Damn it, Ellen, I need you to be here!"

Beside him, the pup whimpered. He'd let her out on a leash to do her business, and now she was wedged up against his leg. "Sorry, pal, looks like we might have to change our holiday plans."

It was then that he heard the sound of a truck negotiating the rutted driveway, which hadn't improved in the short time since he'd left. He watched the red pickup pull over toward the barn. Brake lights flashed briefly when she caught sight of his new 4x4, then the passenger door opened and Pete spilled out, his arms holding a squirming bundle of tan fur.

"Uh-oh. Lady, I think we may be redundant," Spence said softly to the timid creature at his side. The dog he'd called Lady for her gender and delicate features whimpered and leaned against his leg. Reaching down, he scratched her ears.

"Spence! Mom, Spence is here! Hurry!" Pete started running toward the house, clutching a squirming pup in his arms. "I knew you'd come back. Mom didn't believe me, but I told her— Is that your dog? Hey, we've both got a dog now, that's totally cool!"

By that time Pete and the mongrel pup were on the

porch. The two dogs were going through the canine ritual of establishing rank. Ellen stepped down from the truck and stopped, one hand on the door. When she made no move to come closer, Spence left Pete to look after both pups, loped down the front steps and hurried across the clearing before she could change her mind.

"Ellen? I, uh, thought I'd come by and wish you a merry Christmas."

She looked angry. Not a good sign, not good at all. "I brought Pete a surprise, but it looks like I'm a little late. I can pretend she's mine."

Ellen's lips tightened. Her eyes flashed green fire in a face that was so damned dear to him it was all he could do not to clasp it between his hands and kiss her until neither of them could remember what it was she was holding against him.

He knew what he'd like for her to hold against him. Her body, baggy jeans, faded shirt and all.

She continued to look him over, evidently not particularly liking what she saw. He'd showered, shaved and dressed in a suit and tie, even splashed on a palmful of cologne. At the moment he felt distinctly overdressed.

She stared at his boots, which had probably cost more than she spent in feed for all her stock in a month. A lot more. So he did what any good lawyer would do, he created a diversion.

"Things are looking good around here," he said with a smile that had to be forced. He felt cold. Cold and scared. "I see Miss Sara had her foal. A filly? She looks good, too, from what I can see."

Silence. He wouldn't go so far as to call it a chilling silence, but it wasn't exactly warm, either. So he tried again. "The, uh, the Christmas wreath looks good. If

I know Pete, he probably wanted to top the Christmas tree with a Delta Wing jet instead of an angel. Hey, you need a hand unloading anything? I mean, as long as I'm here…'' He figured she'd probably been doing some last-minute shopping, as the stores would be closed tomorrow.

"You're not staying," she said flatly.

"I'm not? I mean, of course I'm not. Wouldn't think of it. Like I said, I just came by to drop off—''

She was struggling to drag a twenty-five-pound sack of puppy food out from behind the driver's seat. Carefully edging her aside, he did it for her.

"To drop off what? That dog? If you had any notion of leaving her here, we already have a dog. We just got back from the pound.''

"Yeah, I see. Looks like Pete's tickled with her. Him. Whatever.''

"As long as you're here, would you mind giving me a hand unloading the bike from the duelly as soon as Pete goes inside? I picked it up from the shop while he was at Joey's house the other day, but it's jammed in behind the seat and I can't get it out.''

"The bike?''

"You know…a bicycle? The thing that got blown away last month?'' She stared up at him, the first hint of concern touching her features. "Spence, what is it? What's wrong? Are you— Is your head—''

"Functioning properly? Evidently not. Yeah, let me give you a hand. Where do you want it, in the tack room?''

Leaving the puppy food on the hood of the pickup, he manhandled the awkward cargo out of the larger duel-wheeled truck. If he was any judge, Pete would outgrow it within the year. Still, it was a sturdy model—nothing fancy, but serviceable. He wheeled it into the barn. Late-afternoon sunlight slanted through the door, picking up dust motes. The place felt good. Felt familiar. Felt like home.

Unaccustomed to being at a disadvantage, he said, "I might as well help you get the stock in as long as I'm here."

"You're not dressed for it."

I can undress. The errant thought popped into his head before he could help himself. Fortunately, he didn't let on that he'd had a momentary vision of the two of them lying naked, limbs entwined on a couple of hundred-pound bales of hay. Be scratchy as the devil, but he had a feeling he wouldn't even notice.

"Spence, do you have time to come in for a minute? I won't keep you long."

If she were a witness, he might have been able to read her, but she wasn't a witness, she was the woman he loved more than he had ever loved anyone or anything in his life. And for the first time he was beginning to realize the gaping hole that would be left in his life if she refused to be a part of it.

"Sure, I'm in no hurry to leave." He leaned the bike against the wall and Ellen reached for a faded horse blanket and moved to cover the Christmas surprise in case Pete got curious when they brought in the stock.

The motion brought her close to where Spence was standing, so close he could inhale the distinctive fragrance of her hair, her soap, the baby powder she used after her shower.

Tucking a corner of the blanket over the handlebar, she said, "Pete made a surprise for you."

"I love you."

"We were going to mail it, but we didn't know your address."

"Did you hear me?"

"You can pretend you think it's great. You don't have to frame it or anything like that...." Her voice trailed off. In the dim light, he caught a glimpse of wetness on her cheek. That was all it took.

"Oh, Ellen, Ellen, don't cry, sweetheart. It's all right. I know I don't have any right to expect— That is, if you did, it would've been great, but since you don't, we can still be friends."

She hit him on the shoulder. Smacked him with her open palm hard enough to rock him back on his heels. "You...you idiot! What's wrong with you? Why didn't you let me know you were all right? It's been five days, and you didn't even call to—"

When he hauled her into his arms and pressed her face against his shoulder, she sobbed out her anger, her fears, her frustrations. He made soft, soothing sounds, things like, "There, there, now. Shh, it's all right."

"Well, why didn't you call?" Lifting her face, she glared at him, wet, red-rimmed eyes, pink-tipped nose and all. Never had he seen a face more beautiful, more beloved.

"I wanted to call at least a hundred times, but, sweetheart, I had to be sure. Del Brio's out on bond, still capable of pulling strings, unfortunately, but not for long. Aside from another mission I've been involved in—I'll tell you about that later—I had to be sure you and Pete were completely safe, and that meant waiting until anyone who thought they could get to me through you was taken care of."

"Taken care of?"

"One way or another. Remember your tattooed

friend, one of Del Brio's goons? He had the misfortune of being involved in a fatal accident. It happened just before he could be called on to testify against his boss.''

''You mean, he was murdered.''

''The terminology varies, but yeah, that's about the size of it. His partner, Silent Sal, apparently fled the country.''

She took it pretty well. Cool, seemingly composed. Then her chin gave one small wobble, and he caught her to him again, pressing her face against his shoulder. Any excuse to hold her in his arms. For a guy who was supposed to be fairly intelligent, fairly well-educated, reasonably experienced in social matters, he was at a complete loss.

For several moments he simply held her there, rocking her gently, savoring the experience while he still could. He'd told her how he felt and she'd ignored him. Case closed.

Damn it, case reopened! ''Look, I don't know if you're interested or not, but I've resigned.''

She gave him a startled look. ''Resigned? What on earth are you going to do?''

''Honey, it was time. Besides, I didn't have a whole lot of choice. Malone, the puppet Del Brio put in place as soon as I was out of the picture, has agreed to testify. That means Frankie is in too much trouble to worry about me, so you see, he's no longer a threat to you or Pete. Now that I've resigned I'm no threat to him, either, and whatever else he is, nobody's ever accused Frank Del Brio of being stupid.''

She was toying with the silver tips of his string tie. At least she hadn't pulled away completely. ''I don't understand. You resigned so that this man wouldn't be able to put pressure on you?''

"Using you and Pete. Right. Honey, it was the only way."

"You resigned because of us. That's not right. You could have gone on to be…well, maybe attorney general, if not governor."

He had to laugh at that. "Whoa! I appreciate the confidence, but believe me, I've never had any political ambitions. Retirement suits me just fine. Besides, I've got other ideas."

"Spence, a minute ago you said…" Her voice trailed off. Her fingers were moving now on the pearl studs fastening the front of his Western-style shirt. "You said something a few minutes ago—"

His pulses ratcheted up a notch. "I did?"

"About—" She broke off and sighed. "I'm just no good at this."

"You're not? I mean, what are you no good at?"

"I don't know how to handle this kind of thing gracefully. I mean, I've been married, for heaven's sake, but I'm still not…I mean, I'm really not very…"

"Experienced. Know something? Neither am I." He was beginning to feel a distinct sensation of warmth creeping into the region of his heart. Other regions, as well. "I know a cure for that."

"For what?" Her face was now pressed against his throat, her hands moving inside his coat, fingers creeping around his waist.

"A lack of experience."

The experience had to wait until much later. Even then, they were aware of the fact that no household was safe from intrusion from an eight-year-old boy on

Christmas Eve. Long after midnight, after the two pups had decided to accept each other's presence in the household as long as Lady was top dog—after an exhausted Pete had shown Spence the drawing he had done for him and accepted Spence's sincere thanks— Spence and Ellen lay in each other's arms on the couch.

"Your ranch is probably so much nicer," Ellen said. He'd told her something about it, not that he'd spent much time there. He'd bought it from a couple of old friends who had wanted to move east to be closer to their children.

"Nah, yours is bigger than mine, if you include your leased acreage. Anyhow, I thought maybe we could keep both, operate them sort of together. Before you know it Pete will be grown up and ready for a place of his own."

"Unless he decides to become a veterinarian or a fighter pilot."

"Even so, he'll need a home base. This can be Pete's. When he's old enough we'll let him decide."

In her chenille bathrobe, her hair still damp from the shower and smelling of green apple shampoo, Ellen traced his features. "I was so afraid to hope," she whispered. "You didn't say you loved me before you left."

"I couldn't afford to take the chance. Sweetheart, you've already lost so much. If I'd told you how I felt and then something had happened so that I couldn't make it back, that would only have made things worse."

"No, it wouldn't."

"You want to fight?"

Eyes gleaming, she shook her head. "You know what I want to do, as soon as we're sure it's safe."

What she was doing to him now was anything but safe, but he didn't have the heart to tell her so. Pete was just going to have to get used to the fact that men and women—daddies and mamas, in particular—needed privacy.

He brought her hand up from his naked chest and kissed her fingertips. In desperation, he rasped, "Want a piece of chocolate pie?"

"Uh-uh. I want a piece of former district attorney, soon-to-be private law consultant, J. Spencer Harrison."

"Sooner than that to be husband of Ellen Wagner, well-known horse breeder, and stepfather to one future artist-astronaut-veterinarian."

From a corner of the cluttered room, a Christmas tree, only slightly lopsided, glowed colorfully. Underneath were packages to be distributed in a few hours. There were still things that had to be worked out, but Spence had no doubt they could do it. Together, they could handle whatever the future brought.

They went into the bedroom but left the radio on in the living room, softly playing Christmas carols as a seasonal cover-up for whatever sounds they might make. Spence would prefer Pete to sleep through the remainder of the night. For a guy who had never known his own father, whose mother had disappeared when he was fifteen, he was surprisingly comfortable with the idea of helping to raise a son, only he'd just as soon get started tomorrow. Tonight belonged to Ellen.

The last carol faded, followed by an advertisement for Hogg's Hardware Emporium, followed by a familiar nasal tenor singing something about an angel flying too close to the earth.

Spence frowned as a half-forgotten memory tripped

a switch in his mind, but then Ellen spoke and everything else disappeared.

"Babies," she said, quietly using her hands to send him into cardiac arrest. "Did I happen to mention I might want some more babies before I get too old?"

He managed to catch his breath sharply as she touched a sensitive place in the crease of his groin. "Just might?" he gasped. "Better make up your mind fast unless you want to wait until I can retrieve something out of the bedside table."

Ellen laughed, a sound that was more beautiful than any song Willie Nelson had ever sung, and then Spence was laughing, too.

Oh, yeah. Retirement was going to suit him just fine.

* * * * *

*Don't miss the next story from
Silhouette's*
LONE STAR COUNTRY CLUB:
*AN ARRANGED MARRIAGE
by Peggy Moreland*

Available December 2002

*Turn the page for an excerpt from this
exciting romance…!*

One

Mission Creek, Texas, was no booming metropolis by any stretch of the imagination. Tucked between Corpus Christi and Laredo, it was originally built to serve the needs of the large ranching community surrounding it. In spite of its modest size and humble beginnings, the town was filled with enough crime, corruption and scandal to keep the scriptwriters for *Law & Order* in new material for years. Perhaps even enough to justify the filming of *Godfather IV*, since the mob was involved in the majority of the shady goings-on around town.

This wasn't the mission Creek Clay Martin remembered from his boyhood, and it certainly wasn't the peaceful environment he'd sought when, disillusioned with life, he'd ended his military career, accepted a job as Texas Ranger and made the long trek back to Texas. But changed or not, it was his home and Clay was determined to do his part in bringing law and order back to the town.

At the moment, though, he was officially off duty and nursing a beer at the bar in the Lone Star Country Club's Men's Grill. The building that housed the bar was a temporary structure built to replace the original Men's Grill destroyed by a bomb several months prior. In spite of its stopgap status, the bar's interior still managed to reflect the taste of the club's wealthy members.

Unfortunately, Clay wasn't one of them.

By all rights, he knew he could be arrested for trespassing. Only card-carrying, dues-paying members were allowed admittance to the prestigious country club's facilities, and Clay didn't have the pedigree or the portfolio to even apply—two small details he didn't see changing anytime in the foreseeable future.

The rich get richer, while the poor keep digging themselves deeper and deeper into debt, he thought with more than a little resentment. That was one thing about Mission Creek that hadn't changed over the years.

With a woeful shake of his head, he drained his beer, then lifted a finger, signaling the bartender to bring him another one. Within seconds a foaming pilsner of beer was sitting in front of him. Clay snorted a laugh as the bartender walked away.

Member or not, it seemed when a Texas Ranger asked for something, it was his for the taking.

With the exception of the money this particular Texas Ranger needed to hold on to his family's ranch.

His amusement faded at the reminder of his current financial woes. Curling his fingers around the glass, he scowled at the golden liquid, wondering how in the hell he was going to come up with the money he needed to turn his family's ranch into a profitable business. If he'd been smart, he'd have socked away more of the money he'd earned while serving in the Special Forces branch of the army. But, no, he'd foolishly squandered his pay trying to impress a wealthy heiress, whom he'd even more foolishly made the mistake of falling in love with.

"Women," he muttered under his breath. "Nothin' but trouble."

"I'll drink to that."

Clay glanced over to find Ford Carson sliding onto the stool next to his, his glass lifted in a silent toast of agreement. Chuckling, Clay tapped his glass against Ford's. "You got women trouble, Mr. Carson?"

Frowning, Ford plucked the skewered olive from his drink and tossed it aside. "Daughter trouble, to be exact."

Clay didn't have to ask which one of Carson's twin daughters was causing him problems. Fiona's escapades were known all over town. "And what has Fiona done this time?"

Ford's face, already florid, flushed an unhealthier red. "The damn girl went out and bought herself a brand-spanking-new Mercedes. Didn't even ask my permission." Dragging a hand over his thick white hair, he shook his head wearily. "I tell you that girl is going to be the death of me."

Ordinarily, Clay would have let the comment pass without comment, but the thought of anyone frittering away tens of thousands of dollars when he was so desperately in need of money infuriated the hell out of him. "If she were *my* daughter, I'd cut off her access to my bank accounts, then march her butt right back down to that dealership and make her return the car."

Ford angled his head to peer at Clay. "You would?"

He gave his chin a decisive jerk. "Damn straight. What she did was totally irresponsible and disrespectful of the privileges you've obviously allowed her."

"And you think that would teach her a lesson?"

Clay lifted a shoulder. "Maybe. Maybe not. Fiona's what? Twenty-seven?" At Ford's nod, he shook his head. "Pardon me for saying so, Mr. Carson, but Fiona's had things her way so long, it may take more than a slap on the hand to bring her around."

Ford's frown deepened. "You're probably right. A headstrong young woman like Fiona won't break easily."

The two stared at their drinks, both absorbed by their own problems. After a moment Ford glanced Clay's way again.

"I heard you bought back your family's ranch."

"Yeah," Clay replied. "But unless I can figure out a way to raise the cash to make the improvements needed to turn the place into a profitable business again, I'm going to lose it."

"I wouldn't toss in my cards just yet," Carson said thoughtfully.

Feeling the man's gaze, Clay glanced up to find Ford studying his reflection in the mirror behind the bar.

"What if I were to give you the money you needed to get started," Ford suggested.

"*Give* me the money?" Clay repeated.

"Well, not *give*," Ford amended. "A little trade."

Clay snorted. "And what would you want of mine in trade?"

"You have traits that I admire. Traits that I'm willing to pay for."

Clay shook his head, wondering if the beer was clouding his thinking, or if Ford Carson truly wasn't making a lick of sense. "Sorry, but I'm afraid I'm not following you."

"I want you to marry my daughter," Carson said, then held up a hand when Clay choked a laugh. "This is no joke, son," he warned. "I'm willing to pay you a hundred thousand dollars, if you'll agree to marry

Fiona for two months and teach her the meaning of responsibility and commitment.''

Clay stared at Carson, unable to believe the man was serious. A hundred thousand dollars? he thought, trying to absorb the magnitude of the offer. A hundred thousand dollars would go a long way toward rebuilding his family's ranch. And all he had to do to get the money was agree to marry Fiona Carson and stay married to her for two months?

It was insane, he told himself. Ludicrous.

"And Fiona will go along with this?" Clay asked doubtfully.

"She won't have a choice," Ford replied confidently, then chuckled. "Of course, she won't know the real purpose of the marriage. She's stubborn. Takes after her old man in that way. If she knew that I'd arranged for you to marry her to teach her responsibility, she'd dig in her heels so deep, it would take a team of Clydesdales to drag her to the altar.''

Frowning, Clay shook his head. "I don't know, Mr. Carson. I need to give this some thought.''

Carson rose and tossed a business card onto the bar. It landed faceup beside Clay's hand. "Take all the time you need. That's my private number. Give me a call when you've made your decision.''